PR

THE HUNDRED L̶i̶e̶s̶ ̶o̶f̶ LIZZIE LOVETT

"Intricate characters whose stories are resonant and memorable."

–Publishers Weekly

"A dark, comedic mystery about a girl's quest for proof that ultimately helps her discover some truths about herself."

–Justine Magazine

PRAISE FOR
AS YOU WISH

"Easy to read and hard to put down."

–VOYA Magazine, Perfect Ten

"Heartbreaking, other times hilarious, but always thought-provoking. An unexpectedly affecting book that will have readers pondering what they would wish for if given the chance."

–Booklist

PRAISE FOR
IT CAME FROM THE SKY

"A balanced exploration of maturity, vulnerability, human connection, and our innate desire to believe."

—Kirkus Reviews

"[A] quirky, intelligent novel...Big questions of morality, cosmic insignificance, and human connection ground this novel even as it ponders the stars."

—Booklist

TELL ME WHAT WHAT REALLY HAPPENED

ALSO BY CHELSEA SEDOTI

The Hundred Lies of Lizzie Lovett

As You Wish

It Came from the Sky

TELL ME WHAT REALLY HAPPENED

CHELSEA SEDOTI

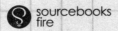

sourcebooks
fire

Copyright © 2022, 2024 by Chelsea Sedoti
Cover and internal design © 2022 by Sourcebooks
Cover design by Liz Dresner/Sourcebooks
Cover images © allanswart/Getty Images, Mizina/Getty Images, Shutterstock/tsuponk

Published by Sourcebooks Fire, an imprint of Sourcebooks
P.O. Box 4410, Naperville, Illinois 60567–4410
(630) 961-3900
sourcebooks.com

Cataloging-in-Publication Data is on file with the Library of Congress.

Printed and bound in Canada.
MBP 10 9 8 7 6 5 4 3 2 1

For E + M

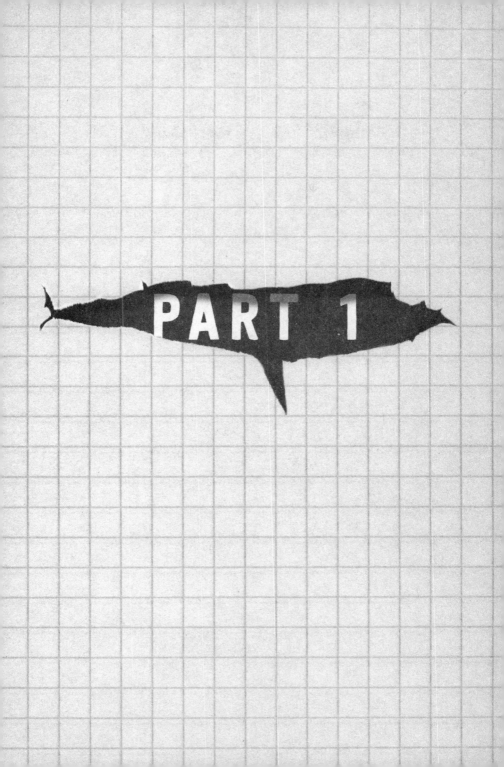

PART 1

We'd like to ask you some questions about
what happened last night. Don't worry; you're
not in trouble. We just want to get to the,
bottom of this. You want that too, don't
you? Great. Please answer honestly and be as
detailed as possible—the more you tell us,
the better our chances of finding Maylee.

PETRA

I don't think you grasp the urgency of the situation, so let me break it down for you, okay?

Maylee Hayes is lost in the woods. She has no jacket. No hiking boots. No GPS—and this is a girl who once got lost going to a Starbucks three blocks from her house. It's got to be...what, two p.m., something like that? So there are only a few hours of daylight left. And you must have noticed that we've got freaking apocalypse-level storm clouds rolling in.

Also—and this is something I *really* shouldn't have to educate you on—the first forty-eight hours are critical when searching for a missing person.

My point is, I don't want to tell you how to do your job. But maybe, *maybe*, instead of sitting here asking me the same questions fifty billion times, you should be looking for Maylee.

NOLAN

Maylee Hayes is dead.

Yeah, sure, I know Petra disagrees. She thinks Maylee's lost and she's pissed we didn't do enough to find her. Last night, in the woods, after...after everything, Petra starts barking out orders: telling Abigail to search the perimeter of that creepy cabin, telling John to wait at the campsite in case Maylee comes back. She tells me to call 911.

I point out that we don't have cell service.

And even though it's so dark I can hardly see Petra's face, I just know she's looking at me like she wants to knock my teeth out. She says something like, "Oh my God, then walk down the road until you *do*, Nolan. Do I really have to lead you through this step by step?"

I start to walk off. That's how screwed up my head is. I actually move through the forest to make the phone call—even though being alone in the woods is beyond dangerous. The only reason I stop is because my feet get all tangled in a patch of ivy. That's when I notice that Abigail and John are standing there like statues.

Petra's like, "Are you hearing me?" She shines her flashlight back and forth between them. They both look like they're maybe gonna cry or vomit at any second. Petra notices, too, because her voice loses its edge. She says, "What's wrong? Someone tell me what's going on."

We don't have time for this. Unless we want to end up like Maylee, we've got to get out of the woods fast. No searching, no wasting time trying to find cell service. We need to *leave*. I try to tell Petra that. I try to tell her what I saw.

Of course, she immediately freaks the fuck out, all, "Don't. Don't you dare start with that trash right now. I will kill you, I swear to God, Nolan, I will *kill* you."

So I stop talking. What else am I gonna do?

Even now, probably at this exact moment, Petra's still telling herself that Maylee is alive out there, taking shelter under a log or something. Saying she'll be found soon enough. But yeah, it's not gonna happen. Maylee is dead.

Yeah, I'm sure.

I'm *positive*.

I saw it happen.

[pause]

It was by the creek. I think. I don't know; I got all turned around. Maylee had run off and the four of us were looking for her. We split up. Petra said not to split up, but no one listened.

So I'm alone, and I hear this noise.

This *wet* sound.

Like when you're cleaning soggy leaves from the gutter and a whole handful of them splats on the ground.

I move toward the sound, pushing through bushes or ferns or whatever they are, wishing it wasn't so dark. My flashlight beam is too weak to cut through the trees more than a few feet. I'm trying to be quiet but snapping twigs with every step. I'm so focused on how much noise *I'm* making, I don't notice the forest has gone weirdly silent. No pine needles rustling, no bugs or birds or other animals.

I should have noticed right away.

I *should* have.

I stumble and reach out to brace myself against a tree, stick my hand in something damp and slick, that disgusting moss that grows on everything around here. I'm in the process of wiping the slime off on my hoodie when I see lights. Two glowing pinpricks hovering in the air. Except they're not *lights*. They're eyes. It's eyeshine reflected from my flashlight beam. *Blue* eyeshine.

I freeze because I know what's happening. I know *exactly* what's happening. I've been reading about this my entire life. It feels like forever, I'm looking at this creature, and I know it's looking back at me.

It breaks eye contact first. Turns back to the ground, back to what it had been doing before I interrupted.

That's when I realize.

Maylee's body is down there. And that wet sound I heard... The creature, it's ripping her apart.

ABIGAIL

Nolan ran up to me and his eyes had turned into hard little marbles, and his mouth was moving but no words came out for the longest time. Then finally he said, "It's eating her. It's *eating* her."

I asked over and over, "What is? *What* is? A bear?"

But he kept shaking his head.

And I asked, "Did you shoot it?"

Because I'd heard the gunshot, you know?

Nolan said no, and he was trembling so bad it was like an earthquake had started in his belly and was jolting through the rest of him. I thought maybe he was having a panic attack. That happened to a lady at Sunny Acres once. She got super scared when her tabby went into labor—the cat was so overweight, the lady didn't even know it was pregnant—and she started to panic, only she thought she was having a heart attack. Before then, I hadn't realized panic attacks were so serious. Kids at school say stuff like "That midterm gave me a panic attack." After the thing with my neighbor, I was always going, "That's not what a panic attack actually *is*, though." But I don't think anyone was probably—

Huh?

Oh, sorry. What was I saying? Right. Okay. So Nolan was shaking and shaking, and his lips went kinda blue, and I wondered if I should call an ambulance, only there wasn't any cell service.

"Just tell me what you saw," I begged him, because I thought if I just knew that part, maybe I could figure out what should happen next.

And Nolan... He tried to tell me. He told me *something*. He wasn't making much sense, though. I guess we were all so scared, probably none of us knew what we were saying.

Besides, it ended up not mattering. Because right then, John stepped out from behind a gnarled fir tree. He had Maylee's blood on his hands.

JOHN

I think I'd like to speak to a lawyer.

1

For our records, please state your full name
and your relationship to Maylee Hayes.

PETRA
Oh my God, you're seriously going to make me do this?

Fine.

My name is Petra Whitfield. That's W-H-I-T-F-I-E-L-D.

Maylee Hayes is my best friend.

Trust me when I say that no one—*no one*—knows Maylee
better than I do.

[pause]

You want me to get into all that? Really?

[pause]

No, I don't mind. I just wonder if, *you know*, there's a more
efficient use of our time. But whatever. Since it's so important
to you:

Maylee and I met on the first day of kindergarten, back when I was this raggedy-ponytailed mess. It was before my dad married Brenda and he tried his hardest, but he wasn't exactly prepared to raise a little girl on his own.

That morning, my class was waiting on the blacktop for our teacher to open the door. *Of course* my dad walked me right up to the group and reminded me twelve times not to leave the premises with anyone but him. Then he triple-checked my list of emergency numbers. You know how he is.

When he finally left, I saw Maylee for the first time. My eyes snapped right to her. It was because of her hair. She had this slippery-looking gold hair pulled back in the neatest French braid I'd ever seen.

It stood out because that's how I'd wanted *my* hair. Every night for a week my dad watched tutorials and practiced French braiding while telling me bedtime stories. He couldn't get it right, though—and honestly, even properly braided, my frizzy brown hair wasn't ever going to look sleek.

I inched closer to Maylee, just to get a better look at her braid. I was mesmerized by its twists. I wanted to reach out and touch it. I almost *did*.

Maylee noticed me then.

I was five, so I didn't feel like a creep. I just real casually said, "I like your braid."

She looked at me harder and was like, "Your hair is messy."

I just nodded because obviously she was right.

Then she glanced down at my rainbow-striped Keds. She said, "We have the same size feet."

We did.

We still do.

Maylee said we should trade one shoe. She didn't even wait for me to respond, just pulled off one of her glittery Mary Janes. The left one. One of the clearest memories of my life is looking down and seeing my rainbow shoe on my right foot and Maylee's shoe on my left.

We walked around like that all day. It felt kinda like an announcement. Kids looked at my feet, then at Maylee's, and thought, "Oh, okay, they belong together."

And we did.

We still do.

[pause]

It's weird: you kind of forget how many good moments you had with someone until...

[pause]

Never mind. I don't even know where I was going with that. Have I mentioned that I haven't slept in like thirty-five hours?

NOLAN

My name is Nolan Anderson. I didn't have a relationship with Maylee. She was my stepsister's best friend. That's all.

PETRA

Yeah, Nolan's my brother.

Stepbrother, technically.

But our parents have been married since I was seven and he was six. We grew up together. It's kinda weird to add some qualifier before "brother."

NOLAN

It's different for Petra: Her real mom died. My parents just divorced. I go to my dad's every third week and alternate holidays. He's remarried, and I have two half brothers. It's cool that Petra wants to act like we're bio siblings, but I'm not gonna ignore a whole other half of my life.

PETRA

Of course Nolan feels the same way about our relationship as I do.

I mean, we've never talked about it or anything, because Nolan's not the sort of person you have big heart-to-hearts with. But some things you just know.

JOHN

My name is John Massey Jr., and Maylee Hayes wa—

[coughs]

Sorry. I'm getting over a cold.

My name is John Massey Jr., and Maylee Hayes is my girlfriend.

ABIGAIL

Maylee was a friend of mine.

A *sort of* a friend, anyhow. Maybe more of an acquaintance. Or someone I used to be friends with? I don't know. It's actually really complicated.

I was excited about the camping trip because I thought, "Oh cool, maybe Maylee and I will get close again." And it was a chance to get to know Petra and John and Nolan. I saw them around school, but that's basically it. Like, before all of this, I'm not sure they even knew my name. So I thought maybe I could make some new friends, you know?

I guess it's not going to work out that way.

Huh?

Oh, right. I'm Abigail Buckley. Or wait, when you say "full name," do you mean middle name, too? Abigail Amelia Buckley, then. The Abigail is for Nana Abbie, and the Amelia is for

Grandma Amelia, who I never actually met because she died before I was born.

My dad says that's what happens when you do drugs, you die way young, and that's the reason I should never touch them. Also because they're really expensive. He always tells me I better not get into that stuff because he won't be paying my debts.

But I wouldn't be interested in drugs anyhow. Not even if I was trying to make a good impression on someone who offered them to me.

Not that I've been in that situation.

Really.

2

How did the camping trip come about?

JOHN

Before we get into this, I want to make something clear.

This isn't my first time in an interrogation room. I know the drill. I know not to talk.

My lawyer, she says innocent people have a long history of talking themselves into prison. They figure they've got nothing to hide, so what's the harm in telling the cops everything, right? But no matter how innocent someone is, if they talk long enough, eventually their words can be twisted—especially when the person in question is a Black boy being accused of murder.

[pause]

My lawyer's not happy I'm saying this to you, I can tell by her expression. She actually advised me to leave—let me know I'm free to walk out of here unless you charge me with something.

But I won't. I'll sit here and answer your questions honestly, cooperate to the best of my ability.

That's *all* I'll do, though. I won't let my guard down. I won't volunteer more than exactly what you asked for. I won't be tricked into incriminating myself.

I love Maylee, and I want you to find out what happened to her, but I've got to protect myself, too.

That's what she would want.

[pause]

With that out of the way, the camping trip was Maylee's idea. I think she originally meant for us to go alone, but Petra invited herself along.

NOLAN

I never asked whose idea it was to go camping. I assume it was Petra's. She's always trying to coordinate camping trips, even though she's the only one who likes them. Well, her and Ray—that's her dad.

Personally, I try to avoid the woods.

Especially the woods around Salvation Creek. I've got an entire file on that place.

PETRA

I love my brother, okay? He's this really great guy in so many ways. But I absolutely *cannot* tolerate his conspiracy theories.

NOLAN

The only reason I was on the camping trip at all is because I was guilted into it. Believe me, the last way I'd choose to spend my time is out in the woods with that group.

I'm just saying, I've got literally nothing in common with them.

PETRA

Honestly, I'm not sure if Nolan *has* friends.

NOLAN

Maylee and John are...I guess [air quotes] popular? Like, maybe not top-tier popular but just below that or something? I don't know. I have no idea how all that hierarchy bullshit works.

JOHN

Maylee's popular, yes. I wouldn't say the same about myself. People only know me from student council and a few different clubs I'm in—yearbook, debate, that kind of thing.

PETRA

Nolan spends almost all of his time online. And I get that he's talking to people on those forums or whatever. But those aren't *real* friends.

NOLAN

My mom and Petra act like online friends are fake. My mom I get. It was different when she was growing up. But Petra? Sometimes I want to shake her and be like, "What *year* do you think this is? Do you know how many people live their *entire lives* through a computer screen?"

PETRA

Sometimes I look at Nolan and think, "One day you're going to look back and realize just how much stuff you missed out on."

NOLAN

Ray is the only one who stands up for me. He tells my mom and Petra to back off. Says, "Don't force Nolan to live the life *you* want." Except, with the camping trip, he completely betrayed me. He's the one who pushed me to go on it.

We talked about it over dinner last... Wow. I was gonna say last week, but I guess it was only three nights ago. That's... Sure, okay. Time feels really weird right now. Anyway, everyone's at the table eating tuna noodle casserole—except for me; I've got a grilled cheese—and Petra mentions camping at Salvation Creek. Ray tenses immediately.

He's not some controlling asshole or anything like that. Just the most paranoid dude I've ever met.

I guess it makes sense—obviously, you know who her dad is.

ABIGAIL

Petra's dad is a cop. That's why *my* dad always told me to steer clear of her. He says not every cop is rotten, but enough are that you should avoid 'em all just to be safe.

[pause]

Oh my gosh, why did I say that to you? Can we pretend I didn't? Sometimes words fly out of my mouth before I even realize it. It's actually super embarrassing.

And anyhow, I'm sure *you're* not bad cops. You've both been nice to me so far. Really.

PETRA

Look, I know my dad is paranoid. But he's been on the force for twenty-five years—working his way up the ranks to lieutenant, as you know, *detectives*. Of course he's paranoid. If most people saw the things he's seen on the job, they would be, too.

JOHN

Yes, I've met Lieutenant Whitfield. He's always treated me...
adequately.

NOLAN

So Ray starts asking all these questions: "Who's going on this
camping trip? What time are you leaving? What time will you be
home? Do you have the GPS coordinates of the campsite?" You'd
think he'd have implanted Petra with a tracking device by now.

That's a thing people do, you know. The government might
not want to talk about it, but I'm just saying, it happens.

Petra's keeping her cool because she's used to this kind
of third degree from Ray. She's prepared with all the right
answers—says she emailed him a file with a map and itinerary and the phone numbers and addresses and probably blood
types of everyone who'll be there.

That's when my mom starts in. She's all, "Nolan, wouldn't it
be fun if you went camping, too?"

Yeah, sure, loads. The same way PE is fun.

I can see from Petra's scowl that she's not thrilled about the
idea, either. Who wants their stepsibling tagging along when
they're trying to party with their friends?

My mom goes into this long speech, basically about how I'm
a failure at life. I spend too much time in my room; I need fresh

air and sunlight. Like I'm a fucking tulip or something. She says I need a change of scenery; I need more social interaction; I need exercise. On and on and on.

And she wonders why I prefer the weeks I'm at my dad's house.

That's when Ray gets involved. He doesn't give two shits about me getting fresh air. But he's like, "If you went on the camping trip, you and Petra could look out for each other."

Meaning *I* could look out for *Petra*.

Here's the thing: Ray worries about school shootings but doesn't make me walk Petra from class to class. He worries about date rapists but doesn't make me escort her to parties. He worries she's gonna text and drive but doesn't make me babysit her when she uses the car—though he literally won't let us leave the house without lecturing about how even texting at stoplights is bad; how our phones better not be in our hands unless the engine is off.

You see what I'm getting at? What's so different about this camping trip that he wants me there to look out for Petra?

Everyone knows the stories about the woods around Salvation Creek. All the girls who have disappeared there. Kinda makes you wonder, huh? Maybe, in his years as a cop, Ray's learned more about the area than he's telling.

ABIGAIL

I never asked whose idea the trip was. Does it matter? Maylee invited me—she's the only one I really knew. I just thought it was great that she wanted to spend time together again.

PETRA

I honestly found the whole situation weird. Maylee's isn't really a camping person. She's not into early mornings or being anywhere she can't post regular status updates. She always says, "What's even the point of doing something if no one knows about it?" So it was strange that she wanted to go camping and even stranger that she wanted to do it in a place where our phones wouldn't work.

[pause]

I mean, *yeah*, I had a theory. Didn't I mention that I know Maylee better than anyone? Let me put it this way: Maylee brought a two-person tent on the camping trip, and she sure wasn't asking *me* to share with her. Both she and John have parents who are home all the time. You see what I'm getting at?

I thought about telling her we didn't need to make a big production out of it. She and John could go, and I'd cover for her if her mom called. But then I thought about the two of them alone at Salvation Creek, and, look, they're not exactly wilderness experts. I was thinking, "God, they'll probably make camp on top of a cougar den or something." They basically needed me there to prevent any disasters from happening.

Which is sort of funny to think about now.

Maybe "funny" isn't the right word.

[pause]

Anyway. I didn't realize Maylee was inviting Abigail Buckley. I didn't even realize she *knew* Abigail. If you would've asked me a week ago, I would've sworn they'd never spoken two words to each other.

If I'd known Abigail was going to be there, I probably wouldn't have pushed so hard for Nolan to come. When I invited him, I was thinking about how awkward it would be, me sitting alone by a campfire while Maylee and John fooled around in their tent a few feet away. I was scrambling to find someone to keep me company.

Besides, I thought it might be nice to spend time with Nolan. I feel like we hardly hang out anymore.

3

Petra, before we go any further, can you tell
us about those scratches on your cheek?

PETRA

Um... They're scratches? I'm not sure what you want me to
say. We were in the woods. I must have gotten hit with some
branches or something. Are they bad? I didn't exactly stop to
admire myself in the mirror before coming here.

[pause]

They're not defensive wounds, if that's what you're implying.

[pause]

Do I need to get my dad in here? Because I was supposed to
be giving you a routine statement, *not* being treated like a person
of interest. Though, now that I think of it, it's pretty convenient
that you waited until he left for Salvation Creek to separate me
and the others.

Here's the thing: My dad is literally the *only* person I trust to lead the search for Maylee. If I have to call him back to supervise this interview, I'm not going to be happy. And if he finds out you accused me of something without him present, he *really* won't be happy, okay?

So why don't you take a minute to think about what's going on here? Are we just giving you statements, or what? You want to go check on the others and give yourselves a chance to—

[pause]

Okay. Good.

Let's proceed, then.

4

Describe the morning of the camping trip.

NOLAN

What does Petra do at nine o'clock on Saturday morning? She starts packing the car. I'm standing in the kitchen, halfway through a bowl of Lucky Charms, and I say, "I thought we weren't leaving for a few hours."

She keeps dragging the cooler through the house and mutters something about how she wants to be prepared.

That's the problem with Petra. She's so obsessed with being prepared that she *over*prepares. So at ten she's stomping around in flannel and hiking boots, like some pissed-off Paul Bunyan, grumbling about how no one else is ready to leave. But, like, we were told we still had an *hour*.

Petra's cool and all...but yeah, she's a lot to handle.

PETRA

I had this whole itinerary. I scheduled our arrival at the campsite for twelve thirty. Not obnoxiously early but plenty of time to guarantee a spot.

There aren't reservations at Salvation Creek; it's backcountry camping. No bathrooms or running water or anything. Whoever shows up first gets the prime camping spots. Granted, I've never actually *seen* other campers there, but there's usually remains of campfires or trash that some jerk didn't pack out.

I also wanted to get there early to maximize the time we spent in the woods. I wasn't overjoyed about a single-day camping trip. Do you know what a *pain* it is to lug gear out there, only to turn around and load it back into the car the next day? I would've preferred to wait until fall break so we could do a longer trip, but Maylee insisted. She wanted to go camping *that* Saturday.

When she told me, I was like, "Um, you mean *four days* from now?"

Maylee's never been much of a planner.

Anyway. Getting to the campsite earlyish shouldn't have been an issue. I figured we'd leave Wilton at eleven and arrive at Salvation Creek by twelve thirty at the latest. Easy.

Except Maylee called me at 10:55. She wanted to know if I remembered to pack the skewers—of course I did—then she said she was about to get in the shower. I was like, "Pardon me? You're supposed to be at my house right now."

Her response was "You know I sleep in on weekends."

I'm not going to lie, okay? I was slightly irritated.

Then Maylee said she'd keep her shower quick, she wouldn't even blow-dry her hair, but she needed to shave. Which caused an argument because, I'm sorry, she can deal with hairy legs for one night.

And she was like, "This is my comfort we're talking about. How am I going to have fun this weekend if scratchy leg hair is causing me physical *discomfort*?"

Look, I'm not hating on Maylee for shaving or painting her nails or doing any other girly crap, because I do it, too. But it would've been nice if she handled her beauty routine on her own freaking time.

JOHN

Maylee texted in the morning to say she was running late— which I'd expected.

[pause]

Why?

Because Maylee's *never* on time.

Petra was upset about it, which I understood. I'm generally

punctual, too. But yesterday, leaving an hour late didn't seem worth getting stressed about. I reminded Petra that we were going camping, not taking the SAT.

NOLAN

An hour passes. Then another. Then *another*. Clearly, things aren't going according to plan, and I'm starting to wonder if maybe I'll get lucky and the whole thing will be called off.

Because yeah, I've been dreading the trip from the second I agreed to go. Even for just one night, I can't see myself sleeping in a tent. Pissing behind a tree. I can't see myself lying there in the dark, listening to the woods around me and hearing that first telltale noise—the sound of two sticks hitting each other. *Crack-crack.*

Petra is pacing up and down the hall, sighing dramatically and looking out the front window, like that's gonna make Maylee show up quicker. I duck into my room to avoid her. It's like midnight in there, even though the sun is shining—thank you, blackout curtains. I turn on my computer, and before I know it, I'm messaging back and forth with this guy from NACRO.

PETRA

Freaking *NACRO*. You know what that stands for, right?

No?

North American Cryptozoology Research Organization.
Yeah. Think about that for a second.

NOLAN

The guy from NACRO, his name is Dave. He's telling me that he was just at Yosemite.

You ever been?

Ray organized a family trip there a couple years ago, but I stayed with my dad that week. I wouldn't go to Yosemite if you paid me. More people disappear under mysterious circumstances there than any other national park.

But that's why Dave is great. Everyone in NACRO knows it's best to stay out of the woods. We're very aware of the risks. But we won't get evidence if *someone* doesn't venture in. That's why Dave travels around the country going to all these nature areas where people have vanished. Or where...you know, where bodies have been found. He's gotten some really interesting footage, and seriously, it'll blow people's minds when he releases it to the public.

PETRA

Finally, at 12:36—yes, I checked the exact time—Maylee called again.

And she said, I swear to you, she actually had the nerve to say, "I'm three minutes from leaving my house. Are you ready or what?"

I was perched on the edge of the couch, tapping my fingers on the armrest, staring at the clock and hoping no one stole my tent from the roof of the car. I told her, "Are you freaking kidding me right now? I've been ready for hours."

Maylee snort-laughed, because *obviously* she was kidding. She knows me as well as I know her; she was very aware that I was angrily trying to redo our entire afternoon schedule.

But the thing is, Maylee also knows her laughter is infectious.

Even though she was late, even though I was annoyed, when she laughed it made me laugh, too.

NOLAN

So I'm telling Dave about the camping trip. And he's saying— well, he's *typing*, but he's saying it to me, you know? He's saying, "Salvation Creek? That's a cluster area."

I say, "You think so?"

Sure, *I've* always thought it was a cluster area, but we're not talking Yosemite or Crater Lake or something. Salvation Creek is just a little patch of woods in the middle of nowhere. I'm shocked Dave has even heard of it.

He says, "I've got a write-up of the activity around there. Goes all the way back to the early 1900s."

It's 1903, to be exact.

He says, "Just a few months ago, a girl disappeared in the area."

He doesn't need to tell me. I know. I *know*.

Here's Dave, one of the *founders* of NACRO, and he's instructing me to take my camera, take a tape recorder, take notes. He's asking if I have a thermal imager, asking if I know how to use it. He's telling me I'll have an inside look at what's happening around Salvation Creek and I shouldn't waste it. On Sunday, when I get home, he wants a report on anything I saw. He says maybe we can set up a phone call.

I'm not into the phone call idea—don't we talk online so we can *avoid* the phone? But that's a problem for future me.

All I can think in the moment is that this important guy is acting like *I'm* the authority. And I realize that if I go to Salvation Creek, I might discover something no one has before. Something that could justify the hundreds of hours I've spent on NACRO's website. Something that would prove to my mom, Petra, Ray, *everyone*, that—

[pause]

Actually, that part doesn't matter. The main thing is that the camping trip suddenly feels less like a burden and more like an opportunity.

ABIGAIL

Maylee said she'd pick me up, which was...fine, I guess. She already knew about me living at Sunny Acres, so it wasn't a big surprise or anything, she'd just never been to my house before. A couple years ago, when we were...when we used to hang out a lot, I always met her somewhere. But like I said, she knew about me living at Sunny Acres, and it's nothing to be ashamed of anyhow. The only reason I feel slightly embarrassed about it is because sometimes kids at school—

Huh?

[pause]

No, I'm not nervous. I guess I'm *a little* nervous because I'm talking to you, and even though I know I'm just giving a statement, talking to the police still kinda makes you feel like a criminal, don't you think? But I'm not *nervous* nervous. Why?

[pause]

Oh, sorry. Nana Abbie always says my mouth needs a pause button. I guess she's right, but I've kinda always thought saying too much is better than saying too little. I'll try to focus, though.

Maylee picked me up in her little lime-colored car. A VW Beetle, one of the newer ones. It was so sparkly, I wondered if she drove through a car wash on the way over. I'm not used to cars that look like that.

She honked once, and I cringed because people just don't drive into Sunny Acres and start honking. It was warm yesterday—warm for October, at least—and everyone had their doors and windows open wide. They came outside to see who was making all that noise in our dusty lot. Maylee's car was the shiniest thing in the whole trailer park. Or maybe Maylee was.

I got into the car fast before anyone could ask questions. I had to kinda wedge myself in—it's not a car made for tall people, you know? Even in the front seat, it felt like my knees were pushed all the way to my armpits. Plus, I was trying to fit my puffy jacket on my lap, and the wind had blown my hair into my mouth, and when I tried to push it away, a piece snagged on my charm bracelet. Maylee sat there watching me, and I was sure she was thinking I was the most awkward person on the planet, but instead she smiled and said, "I'm so happy you're coming."

I told her I was, too.

There were all these other things I wanted to ask her, like if she was excited for the trip and if she thought everything was going to go okay and if—Well. A lot of stuff. But before I could, Maylee put the car in drive and screeched out of Sunny Acres, pulling onto the main road so fast that her hair swished around her shoulders.

I asked if we were in a hurry, and she said, "I'm late. Petra will be in a rage by now."

I shifted, trying to get comfortable on the slippery leather seat, and said, "Really? Does she get mad at you a lot?"

Maylee said, "Only when I don't follow her rules." And she laughed in this way where I couldn't tell if she was joking or not.

She must have been joking.

Don't you think?

Anyhow, after that, Maylee turned up the radio and sang along. Her voice wasn't that great, but you kinda didn't notice. Some people are like that, you know? They don't need be good at any specific thing because just being *them* is talent enough. I swear, Maylee would've been famous if she hadn't...

[pause]

No, I'm okay. Actually, sorry, yes, a tissue would be good. Thank you.

[pause]

We were on the road, and I asked Maylee if we were going straight to Petra's. She said we had to pick up John first. I must have made a weird face or something. I don't *remember* making a face, but my dad always says I'm an open book, even when I think I'm being real good at hiding something.

Maylee glanced over and asked if there was a problem.

I told her no. I just didn't realize John was going with us. But of course she'd invite her boyfriend on the trip; I just... I hadn't realized, that's all.

Maylee reached over and put her hand on top of mine. It stopped my words right up. She said, "John's a great guy. Give him a chance, okay?"

I said okay. And I did give him a chance. I tried, at least. Because I knew Maylee wouldn't date someone awful. It's just... It's hard to talk to John without thinking of what happened at the beginning of junior year. The accident. I know he was never arrested, and it was supposedly all a big misunderstanding. But...I don't know. Sometimes I wonder.

JOHN

Before the camping trip, Abigail and I had only spoken a few times. I got the impression she didn't like me much.

[pause]

No, I don't know why—not for sure.

But based on what I've seen of her family, I wouldn't be surprised if it had to do with the color of my skin.

PETRA

Maylee finally rolled up to my house at one o'clock. She got out of the car, then John got out of the car, then *Abigail Buckley* got out of the car. And I was like, pardon me? Who even *is* this person?

Yes, I'm exaggerating. I knew who she was, we've been in school together forever. But no one *really* knows her. She's this random girl who lives in the trailer park on the west side of Wilton. Not that there's anything wrong with the trailer park; I'm sure there are plenty of great people there. But *her* family...

Let me break it down for you, okay? You've probably seen her dad's truck around town—you know, the lifted pickup leaving a trail of tobacco juice in its wake. The body is patched together with random junkyard panels, and there are flagpoles, actual *flagpoles*, on either side of the bed with American flags waving from them. The tailgate is covered with bumper stickers that say crap like *Keep honking, I'm reloading* and *Fear the government that fears your guns*. Then there's my personal favorite part: across the back window, an enormous decal that says *Hillbilly Supreme*. And I'm like, why? Just *why*?

My point is this: If you drive a truck like that, you're basically telling the world everything they need to know about you. And yeah, I get that Abigail isn't her dad. But let's just say people carry their upbringing wherever they go.

So while I stood there looking at Abigail—wondering what the crap she was doing at my house and why she was wearing an enormous jacket when it was seventy freaking degrees out—Maylee waved and started pulling bags from her VW. She said, "I know I'm a little late."

Try *two hours* late.

There was no point making a big thing of it, though. Maylee would've just shrugged and tossed out something infuriating like "We'll get there when we get there." Whatever. I had bigger concerns at the moment.

The cooler was still on the porch, and I told Maylee to help me with it. John was like, "Hey, I'll grab that for you."

So I had to super quickly tell him no thanks, we had it covered. I ignored his baffled expression and motioned for Maylee to follow me. As soon as we were out of earshot, I whispered, "What's Hillbilly Supreme doing here?"

Maylee was like, "Wow, Petra. Rude."

I pointed out that it was literally written on Abigail's dad's truck. *Literally.*

Maylee stopped and stared at me for a long moment, blinking her mascaraed lashes. She said, "Yeah, her *dad's* truck. Your dad drives a police car; does that make you a cop?"

I said, "That's different."

I walked up the creaky porch steps, opened the front door, and shouted to Nolan that we were finally leaving. Then I turned back to Maylee and asked how she'd even started talking to Abigail.

Maylee said, "She's in my English class."

Okay, fine. But, like, maybe a little heads-up that she'd be inviting random classmates on the camping trip? And yes, I realize I invited Nolan. But that was different.

We were both quiet for a second. Sometimes we play this game where it's almost like we're daring the other person to talk first.

I always win.

Maylee leaned down and grabbed one side of the cooler, lifting it a few inches off the porch, and was like, "Jeez, this weighs a million pounds. What's in here?"

I said, "Food. You *would* like to eat on this camping trip, wouldn't you?"

I picked up my own side. It wasn't the least bit heavy.

Wanna hear something messed up? Last year a girl from school asked if it's hard to be Maylee's friend because she's so pretty. I was like, "Um, *no*," because why should that even matter—and by the way, thanks for basically calling me ugly.

It's *not* hard, though. I literally never think about it. I mean, yeah, I obviously don't look like Maylee. No one's ever going to call me dainty and adorable. But you know what? I'm fast and strong, and I can lift a freaking cooler.

Anyway.

Maylee glanced back toward her car. Abigail still stood by the dusty VW in that awkward, hunch-shouldered way of hers while John tried—and failed—to engage her in conversation.

I was about to break the silence when Maylee sighed and said, "Look, some guys have been bullying Abigail. Chase Edwards and Robbie Martinez, mostly. You know how I hate seeing that. So I just wanted her to feel like...I don't know. Like not all humans are bad."

She shrugged and reached back to adjust her braid. The collar of her slouchy sweater slipped off her shoulder, and I considered pointing out that she'd clearly disregarded my advice on wilderness attire.

Instead, I said, "Okay, I get it."

I started moving toward the car, and Maylee was forced to follow, the cooler between us bumping against our knees.

So do you understand now? Sometimes Maylee can be inconsiderate and frustrating. But she's also a really great person. And maybe, in a way, I *like* that she's not easy to be friends with.

Because, let's face it, I'm not exactly easy, either.

JOHN

Yes, I'm aware that Maylee has some undesirable qualities.

People point that out to me like it'll come as a shock. Like I somehow didn't notice that my girlfriend can be thoughtless—or whatever it is you're getting at.

Obviously, I've noticed.

But Maylee has good qualities, too.

Great qualities.

[pause]

Before last year, I'd spent my whole life hanging around these academic kids whose lives are completely focused on getting into the right college. That's what my parents pushed for. They've been talking to me about *the future* since I was in elementary school.

But Maylee...she lives in the *present*. She does what feel right, not what other people expect from her. She makes every moment count.

When she and I started dating, that was exactly what I needed.

ABIGAIL

John kept trying to talk to me while we were standing by the car. He was saying...I don't even know. I think he made a joke about how I looked more prepared for the woods than him? Which I guess was true, because he was wearing this nice button-up shirt, and I forget what he had on his feet, but they weren't hiking boots.

I didn't really respond. Not because I was trying to ignore him, I was just super distracted by Maylee and Petra. They'd gone to the porch, where I couldn't hear their conversation, but both of them seemed irritated—which was awkward, because they were definitely talking about me. I started thinking I should have just stayed home and read all weekend. Though, I'd just finished a book I really loved, and you know how sometimes you don't want to start a new book because you're still stuck in the world of the last one?

No? Never? Gosh, you're missing out.

Anyhow. Even though I was feeling really uncomfortable, I knew it didn't change anything. I'd be going on the camping trip whether Petra liked it or not. But I guess it would have been nice if Maylee had told her I was coming earlier.

I would have preferred they'd argued when I wasn't standing right there, that's all.

JOHN

While Maylee and Petra worked out whatever they needed to, I tried asking Abigail if she'd heard anything about a storm coming in. It was still sunny in Wilton, but I'd noticed dark clouds to the east.

PETRA

There's no way Maylee's VW would have made it to Salvation Creek—that car is impractical under the most ideal circumstances; it *definitely* couldn't have handled the unpaved road leading to the campsite. Luckily, my mom—*step*mom, if you want to be technical—said I could borrow her SUV.

My gear was already packed, so we started pulling bags from Maylee's trunk and wedging them into mine.

Nolan came outside while we were doing it. He had a duffel bag in one hand, and you know what he did next?

He stood there.

He stood there on the porch and watched the rest of us load the car.

ABIGAIL

I know it's really bad to judge someone on a first impression— though I guess it's weird to call it a first impression when you've known *of* the person for years and years. But Nolan talks in school even less than I do, so though I'd seen him before, the only thing I knew about him was something Maylee told me about a prank his Boy Scout troop played on him a long time ago.

Anyhow, I was trying not to judge him before he said a word, but he was making it kinda hard, because—

Wait. When you take breaks from talking to me, it's because

you're getting statements from the others, right? Are you...are you telling them what I said in here? Because I'd feel really bad if you repeated this.

[pause]

Okay, good.

What I was going to say is that while the rest of us were loading the car, Nolan didn't help. And it seemed kinda rude to me, that's all. My dad always says you shouldn't ever let another person do your work for you.

NOLAN

I go outside to load the car, and John immediately starts in like we're old pals, all, "Hey, Nolan, it's been a while. How's life? What classes are you taking this semester?" Maylee notices my duffel bag and sneers. She says, "You're not seriously coming with us, are you?" Meanwhile, Petra's shouting out orders like she's commanding an army.

So yeah, I'm feeling overwhelmed. The camping trip hasn't even started, and I already need to catch my breath.

JOHN

I hadn't known Nolan was going on the trip, but I was glad to see him. We hadn't talked much since middle school, back when we were in Scouts together. I knew he'd gotten into some weird stuff since then—

[pause]

What kind of stuff?

I'm not sure what to call it. Paranormal conspiracies, or something? I won't judge the guy's hobbies, though. When I was a kid, I spent an entire year building a to-scale model of a medieval castle, so to each his own.

I was just thinking it'd be cool to catch up with him.

PETRA

Roughly five years after our scheduled departure, the car was *finally* packed and ready to go. But of course Maylee couldn't leave without documenting it. She was like, "Just one picture, okay?"

It's never just one.

But whatever.

Maylee told everyone to stand by the car. Nolan said, "I don't want my picture on your socials."

She was like, "Believe me, no one wants that."

NOLAN

Maylee hands me her phone and tells me to take pictures of the rest of the group. The whole time she's asking if everyone's in frame, if anyone blinked, if there's harsh shadows or blown-out areas.

I keep saying we're all good; everything looks great.

[snort]

As if I'm actually putting effort into it.

Sorry, but I'm not interested in being someone's unpaid social media photographer.

PETRA

After Maylee got her pictures, we climbed into the car. It was a tight squeeze. I was glad I wasn't in the back—between Abigail and John, legroom was basically nonexistent. Nolan sat in the passenger seat and popped earbuds in before his door was even shut. Apparently, that didn't block us out enough, because a second later, he pulled up the hood of his sweatshirt.

Before I even turned the engine on, John was like, "Is everyone buckled?"

I get it, I do. And I'd never complain to him about his paranoia because it's obviously justified. But I was thinking, "Could you give me two seconds, please?"

ABIGAIL

John asked twice if everyone had their seat belts on, and that actually made me feel a little better about him. Or maybe it made me feel sad for him. I don't know.

I clicked my seat belt together, and it was weird because I was thinking that probably no one had told me to buckle up before. My dad never enforced that rule. When I was little, he even let me ride around in the bed of his truck all the time. I'd have to duck down if I saw police cars—That's okay to say now, right? I don't do it anymore. Not after the time my dad got ticketed.

Anyhow, after everyone was buckled, Petra started the car, and we headed toward Salvation Creek. In the front, she and Nolan started arguing—something about the GPS, maybe? In the back seat we were all squished together, so close I could smell Maylee's rose-scented body spray.

Her elbow bumped mine as she scrolled through her photos. She was like, "Seriously, Nolan? Were you *trying* to take shitty pictures?"

She held out the phone to show John, and he said, "You look great in this one. It's a little off-center, but you can crop it."

Maylee didn't seem super convinced, but she thanked John and posted the picture anyway. She tagged all of us—our phones buzzed at the same time. I didn't say anything about it, but I guess it made me feel a little weird. My dad always tells me to be careful what I put online. It's not a good idea to let the whole world know where you're going to be.

5

At that point, were you aware that
someone had brought a gun?

JOHN

[pause]

My lawyer advises me not to answer that question.

NOLAN

Who told you about the gun?

ABIGAIL

It wasn't me, if that's what you're asking. I can see why you'd
think so, but I swear the gun wasn't mine.

[pause]

Do you have it? Because I should probably say that if you *do* have it and you dust it for fingerprints, mine will be there. The gun wasn't mine, but I held it.

Everyone did.

PETRA

Stop being coy and saying *someone* brought the gun. You know exactly who brought it.

God. It's like you're *trying* to waste my time.

6

Prior to the camping trip, were you familiar with the area around Salvation Creek?

JOHN
I'd never been to Salvation Creek before. Camping and hiking isn't really my thing.

[pause]

Yes, I mentioned Boy Scouts earlier—but I'd only joined because my parents thought it'd look good on college applications. I quit when I started high school and picked up other extracurriculars.

My thinking is, humans built civilization to *escape* the wilderness, right? So why would I want to go back into it?

PETRA
Salvation Creek is remote, but that's the point. I obviously don't go into the woods because I want to be around *people*.

You get there by driving northwest from Wilton until there's nothing left but forest. The last thing you pass before the turnoff to the campsite is this seventies-era convenience store. You know the place—weeds growing between gas pumps, signs on the building advertising ice-cold Bud Light and live bait.

NOLAN

There's a sign on the side of the gas station that says *Welcome to Bigfoot Country*.

I'm just saying.

PETRA

Past the convenience store, you start to see turnoffs. Most of them lead to cabins. Not cabins like at Royal Lake, near Wilton—those are million-dollar summer homes designed to look rustic, as if they aren't all rigged up with smart lights and wireless speaker systems. The cabins around Salvation Creek are *actually* rustic. They're meant for hunting. Primitive, you know? Most of them don't have running water or electricity.

One of the turnoffs is marked by a wooden post. No street sign or anything, just a waist-high piece of wood jutting from the ground. The trees grow so close you can hardly see the gravel road past them. It looks like whatever is down that path was abandoned a long time ago.

But that's it. That's the road to the campsite.

ABIGAIL

I hadn't been to that campsite before. I don't think so, at least. I don't want to lie to you and say I've never been there when maybe it turns out my dad took me there once when I was like eight and I just don't remember it. So *maybe* I'd been to the campsite. But probably not.

I was familiar with Salvation Creek, though.

NOLAN

I'll tell you the only thing you need to know about Salvation Creek: it swallows people.

PETRA

Come on. Show me a forest where people *haven't* disappeared.

ABIGAIL

Nana Abbie says the woods around Salvation Creek are haunted; that's why you shouldn't ever wander alone. She says it goes all the way back to how the creek got its name. See, a long time ago, there was a group of travelers who came to the area. They got lost in the woods during the longest stretch on record without rainfall. The whole forest was bone-dry, and the travelers ran out of water.

They wandered for days, only half alive. Then one sunset, they heard the sound of the creek. They were so glad that they fell to their knees and gulped down the water until their bellies were full. They named it Salvation because that's exactly what it was.

Only it turned out the creek water was bad. The travelers got sick. By the next morning, all of them were dead.

But the name Salvation Creek stuck around.

PETRA

Yes, I know the rumor of how Salvation Creek got its name.

Moral of the story: don't drink from a water source unless you know it's potable.

Rookie mistake.

ABIGAIL

Though come to think of it, if all the travelers died, how did anyone find out what they'd named the creek?

NOLAN

It doesn't matter how the creek got its name. What's important is that in 1903 a fourteen-year-old girl vanished into the woods. It's the first recorded disappearance in the area. But definitely not the last.

JOHN

I only know about one disappearance around Salvation Creek: the woman last spring. Jenna something.

NOLAN

The victims are always girls.

    They always vanish in a split second.

    It always appears that they straight up walked away.

    Like something in the woods called to them.

ABIGAIL

Jenna Creighton, that was...gosh, I guess about six months ago? We didn't know each other or anything, but her aunt lives at Sunny Acres, so I felt kinda connected to her. I even donated some money to the fundraiser to help with the search. Only like five dollars because I don't have much spending money, just what Mrs. Chang gives me for watering her plants when she visits her son in Portland, which isn't even that often. But probably every little bit helps, right?

NOLAN

Let's talk about twenty-four-year-old Rose Zelinski, vanished in 1933. She's berry-picking with her husband near Salvation Creek. He turns away for a minute, and when he looks back, she's gone.

The only trace of her ever found is her clothes folded neatly on the side of the path.

The official report states she was killed by a mountain lion. But her clothes weren't *torn* off.

Tell me: You ever seen a mountain lion that knows how to work buttons?

PETRA

I didn't donate money to the Find Jenna Fund because, hello, that's what the police were already trying to do. But I did volunteer to help with the search. My dad was working the case, so I guess it felt kinda personal to me.

Of course, he wouldn't actually let me go out with the search party—he said I was too young. But I helped out with other things, like handing out bottled water to the SAR team. The last thing you need during a search and rescue is someone passing out from dehydration.

NOLAN

How about nineteen-year-old Stephanie Yoshida, 1972? She's with a photography group and says she's stepping off the trail to get a photo of the creek. No one sees her again.

A year later, hunters find her remains four miles from where she went missing. All that's left are her feet and tibia—that's shinbones. They're still in her hiking boots, sticking straight up. As if she was standing there and the rest of her melted away.

You know what they *don't* find? Her camera. I'm supposed to believe that, what, her metal camera decomposed?

ABIGAIL
Do I think...what?

[pause]

I don't know. I guess Jenna Creighton's disappearance has some things in common with Maylee's. She was only a few years older than us. And she was camping with her friends at Salvation Creek—not in the same spot we were, but close. And yeah, she said she was just going to the bathroom and she'd be right back, but...

[pause]

I guess it's similar, but that doesn't have anything to do with anything, does it?

[pause]

Besides, there are *lots* of similar disappearances at Salvation Creek. Nolan told me about a bunch of them.

NOLAN

Want another? Okay, nine-year-old Tina Anthony, 1986. Hiking with her dad, disappears when he checks his map.

The next day a helicopter spots her body on a ridge sixteen miles away. Can you explain how a nine-year-old manages to walk *sixteen miles*, over rough terrain, overnight? Can you explain why the coroner was never able to determine cause of death?

PETRA

I knew they weren't going to find Jenna Creighton alive. Not after forty-eight hours had passed. If you're lost in the woods for that long, there's basically no hope. Still, it was upsetting when my dad told me they were bringing in cadaver dogs. He says the hardest thing about lost hikers is knowing that at any moment a SAR could turn into a body recovery.

NOLAN

What about seventeen-year-old Jessica Gonzales, 1998? She's meeting a group of friends at a campsite—the same campsite we stayed at. Only she never shows. Three days later Jessica's car is found six miles down the main road, just past the convenience store. It's pulled to the shoulder and nothing looks disturbed. Jessica's camping gear is still in the trunk. Her keys are in the ignition.

Then, a full *eleven* days after Jessica disappears, she's found. Alive.

She doesn't know why she left her car. She doesn't know what happened to her in the woods. She doesn't know how she stayed alive without food and water for eleven days—in fact, she insists she was only gone for *two* days.

Explain that to me, why don't you?

PETRA

So let's be real for a minute, okay?

You're asking about Jenna Creighton because, duh, there are similarities between her and Maylee's disappearances. Right?

Okay, cool, cool. At least we've agreed on that.

Now my next question:

If you're so concerned about Maylee and Jenna sharing the same fate, how about you put a little more energy into the search effort and less into this conversation? How about you actually let me go out there and *help*?

JOHN

Creighton, right. Jenna Creighton.

I can't believe I forgot her name—the whole town was obsessed with her disappearance. Maylee was constantly reading articles and watching news clips. She even followed the missing woman on social media. Seemed kind of morbid to me, but I don't know, maybe that's what people do these days.

ABIGAIL

But really, even though it seems kinda similar, what happened to Maylee and Jenna Creighton was completely different.

Jenna got lost and died of hypothermia.

Maylee was *murdered*.

7

Let's get back to yesterday afternoon. What
time did you arrive at Salvation Creek?

ABIGAIL

We got to the campsite around two o'clock.

NOLAN

I don't know when we got there. Late afternoon, I guess. Four
o'clock or something? It must have been pretty late because we
were on that dirt road for a fucking lifetime.

ABIGAIL

Or maybe it was a bit later than two?

Yeah, actually, now that I'm thinking of it, I was kinda hungry
when we were setting up the tents, so it couldn't have been *too*
close to lunchtime, because I don't get hungry right after lunch,
obviously.

PETRA

We got to the campsite just after three. Believe me, I was looking at the clock.

ABIGAIL

On the other hand, I might have skipped lunch yesterday. Did I? I bet I did, because I was nervous and I have this thing where it's really hard for me to eat when I'm nervous.

Huh?

Oh. Just...just about the camping trip and hanging out with people I don't really know. Don't you get nervous about that kinda stuff?

So, right, if I skipped lunch, I would've been hungry earlier, so it was probably close to two after all.

JOHN

I remember glancing at my phone as we were climbing out of the car. It was almost two thirty.

PETRA

Can I ask why you're so focused on when we got there? I mean, that was *hours* before Maylee went missing. What does it freaking matter?

8

Walk us through what happened once
you arrived at the campsite.

ABIGAIL

The dirt road was so bumpy it made my whole body vibrate. Even when we parked and got out of the car, I still felt wobbly for a second, kinda like stepping off the Shake Up at the spring carnival. You've stopped moving, but your body doesn't realize right away, you know?

So my legs were jittering, and I was feeling kinda awkward from being packed in a car with mostly strangers, and I was hungry and worried my stomach might rumble. I get the loudest stomach rumbles, and it's so embarrassing, especially when it happens somewhere like church or in the middle of taking a test.

Maylee stretched her arms above her head and took a deep breath. Then she nudged John and said, "See, this place is totally worth the drive."

John laughed and was like, "I'm still partial to indoor plumbing and electricity, but, yeah, it's nice here."

We'd pulled into a clearing surrounded by fir trees that shot straight to the sky. The air had just the right amount of crispness, and even though I couldn't see the creek because it was down a hill, I heard water moving over rocks. All the tension went right out of my body in a great big *whoosh*.

The woods always make me feel scrubbed clean. It's been that way since I was little and my dad started taking me out with him during the season. He says sunshine and fresh air are the best cures for stress. That and taking down a bull elk with a .300 Win Mag.

Anyhow, what I mean is, when I got out of the car and soaked up that clean piney smell, my nerves melted away, and I felt really, really sure that everything was going to be all right.

PETRA

The sun was basically setting by the time we made camp.

[pause]

Okay, fine, I'm exaggerating. But it *was* late, and I was trying not to be annoyed about it. Everyone jumped in to unload the cars—pulling out sleeping bags, lugging tents over to a fire ring some other campers left. Everyone except Nolan. Instead, he strolled over to me and, I kid you not, said, "Is there anything to eat?"

I was like, "No, Nolan, I organized this entire camping trip but didn't bring any food."

He rolled his eyes, like *I* was the one being a pain, and said, "I mean is there anything to eat *right now*? Anything I can grab real quick?"

I asked if he could wait twenty minutes, and he whined that he didn't get a chance to eat lunch. Um...excuse me? He didn't *get a chance*? What about all that time we were waiting for Maylee and he was in his cave doing whatever Unabomber crap he does in there?

What?

No, I don't *literally* mean he's making bombs. God. I'm supposed to trust your detective skills when you can't even recognize sarcasm?

[pause]

But *anyway*. Nolan was standing there staring at me pitifully, and you know what I did? I'm actually proud of this, because I *could* have told Nolan that he had hours to eat before we left— he could have even brought a snack in the car. I could have told him that it's amazing he's managed to live seventeen years and still be unable to perform basic tasks like feeding himself unless someone put food in front of him.

But I didn't say that.

I just walked away.

NOLAN

At the campsite everyone starts unpacking, but I'm real hungry, you know? I hadn't eaten before leaving because I didn't want to risk running into Petra in the kitchen—she was so pissed about Maylee being late, I knew the odds of her taking it out on me were high. So I dig around in my bag and grab a granola bar, eat it real quick while unpacking the car.

JOHN

I hadn't set up a tent in five years, right? Turns out it's not a skill that sticks with you. But Maylee and I had a good time laughing at how useless we were. That's the type of person she is—she can even make failing at something feel like fun.

PETRA

We set everything up around the fire ring, our three tents making a triangle. After I got myself situated, I walked over to Maylee and John.

They were sort of a hot mess. John was holding the rain fly, looking at it like he'd finally encountered a math problem he couldn't solve. Maylee wasn't much better off. She kept messing up—assembling the poles wrong, fumbling with the tent stakes.

Which, okay, Maylee's not exactly Survivorman, but last I checked, she could put up a standard dome tent. I watched her without saying anything for a second because something was clearly weird. I could feel this nervous energy rolling off her.

John said he was grabbing a bottle of water from the cooler and asked if we wanted anything. I said no. As soon as he was out of hearing range, I said, "Okay, what's your deal?"

Maylee looked me in the eye and said, "I don't know what you're talking about."

As if she hasn't been my best friend forever. As if I wouldn't know better than anyone when something was wrong with her.

But I think it's messed up to make people talk before they're ready, so I let it go.

ABIGAIL

I heard a little of Petra and Maylee's conversation. Poor Maylee. Petra asked if Maylee was okay, and even though Maylee kept saying yes, *yes*, Petra wouldn't stop bugging her.

JOHN

I didn't notice Maylee acting strange—but I'm not always the best judge of her moods.

[pause]

What do I mean by that?

Like...sometimes I'll hang out with Maylee all day thinking everything's great, but later find out she was mad the whole time because I hadn't responded to a text the night before.

[pause]

Or a while back, there were a couple days when I thought something was wrong—it seemed like Maylee was trying to avoid me. I was pretty sure a breakup was coming. Turned out she was planning a surprise for our six-month anniversary. She took me to my favorite burger place, made a cake from scratch. Even bought me a copy of this sci-fi book I'd mentioned wanting to read.

[pause]

I hadn't gotten her anything. Didn't even know we were celebrating six months. Maybe that's the kind of thing I'm supposed to know without being told? Maylee wasn't upset, though. She'd just wanted to do something nice for me, she said, wasn't looking for anything in return.

It *was* nice.

Made me feel really loved.

[pause]

I'm getting off track.

The point is, I'm not great at reading Maylee. If something was weird with her yesterday, Petra's the one to ask. Maylee tells her everything.

PETRA

I asked Maylee and John if they wanted me to set their tent up for them. John laughed and said, "Have a little faith, Petra. We've nearly got it figured out."

He was wrong, but whatever. I went over to check on Nolan and Abigail instead. They were just finishing Nolan's tent. It seemed like Abigail did most of the work, which admittedly made me respect her.

When I walked up, she was using a fist-sized rock to pound the final stake into the ground. Nolan was crouched down next to her and did this elbow nudge thing and said...oh God, I hate to even repeat it. He said, "Wow, you're getting pretty in-tents with that. Get it? In *tents*."

Let me tell you something about my brother: he's the sort of person who should never attempt to tell a joke.

He looked so pleased with himself, too, which made me embarrassed for him. Abigail laughed politely but looked like she was trying to find an escape route. Then I realized Nolan wasn't just joking. He was *flirting*.

Which, like, good on him for finally having the courage to speak to a girl. But *Abigail*? Come on.

How did he not know he was barking up the wrong tree?

NOLAN

Setting up the tent, it's the first I've really talked to Abigail. We're working together quickly, joking the whole time. I guess we kinda click.

And yeah, maybe I'm noticing how pretty she is. Strange-pretty. Like a really gorgeous alien or something. Maybe I'm thinking that I know she's dated girls, but that doesn't mean she's not into guys, too, right?

But that makes it sound like the whole thing is some creepy hookup plot, and it's not like that. That's not why I'm being friendly to her. It's more because Abigail seems as out of place on the camping trip as me. Like we're both awkwardly looking around and thinking, "How the hell did I end up here?"

ABIGAIL

Nolan was actually super nice. I hadn't expected that, because at first he was so quiet, and sometimes quiet people are kinda grouchy. And when I'm around people like that, all the quietness makes me antsy, so I start talking to fill the space, and that makes the quiet person even *more* grouchy.

But anyhow, once Nolan started talking, I realized I was wrong about him. He was actually really sweet and funny.

PETRA

I wanted to save Nolan from embarrassing himself more, so I said, "Are you finished setting up over here?"

Nolan did this salute and said, "Yes, Commander."

Yeah, hilarious.

I told him he should be grateful *someone* was keeping track of the schedule.

He rolled his eyes and was like, "It's a vacation, Petra. We don't need a schedule." And then he looked at Abigail and said—

NOLAN

My mouth opens and I'm not thinking about what I'm about to say. The words just spill out.

PETRA

"If you share Petra's tent, she'll probably try to schedule your dreams. Maybe you should sleep with me instead."

NOLAN

I instantly regret it. It sounds like a proposition, and that's not how I meant it, I swear. I glance at Abigail, and she's got this look of sheer mortification on her face.

ABIGAIL

When Nolan made that joke, I realized...okay, this is going to sound silly, but I guess I assumed I'd be sleeping with Maylee? She didn't tell me to bring my own tent. I don't even *have* my own tent. I've never needed one.

I should've figured it out when Maylee and John started setting up together. I was trying not to watch but kept getting glimpses from the corner of my eye of them laughing and kissing and taking selfies. They were just...I don't know. Really wrapped up in each other, like the rest of us weren't even there.

But even with all that, I *still* thought I'd be the one sleeping in her tent. It wasn't until Nolan's comment, when he assumed I was bunking with Petra, that I realized, oh. Duh. Maylee is sharing a tent with *John*.

It's so obvious now.

Do you ever feel embarrassed over something you think, even though no one knows you were thinking it? Because what if there's this really small chance mind reading is real and someone *does* know your thoughts and they're secretly laughing at how pathetic you are?

That's how I felt right then.

Also, it made me wonder, if I wasn't in Maylee's tent, where *would* I be sleeping?

NOLAN

I want to fix this. I want to reassure Abigail, convince her I'd meant it as a joke. But everything I think to say feels like digging a deeper hole.

JOHN

Maylee and I were just about finished with our tent when she nodded at the others and said, "Looks like drama over there."

She was right, there was obviously some tension. I told Maylee it wasn't our business—but I kept an eye on the situation in case someone needed to step in. I have two younger sisters. I've gotten real good at being a mediator.

PETRA

Abigail had this awful lost-puppy look on her face. I get that Nolan's comment was cringey, but she looked ready to cry. I was like, "Ignore Nolan. He's oblivious, not creepy."

For a second she looked baffled. Then she said, "It's not that. I just realized...gosh, this is going to sound silly, but I just realized I forgot to bring a tent."

NOLAN

Petra just straight up tells Abigail something about how I don't *mean* to be creepy.

Cool. Thanks, sis.

ABIGAIL

All my nature-peace was gone. Not so much because I didn't have a spot to sleep, but because I knew Petra and Nolan and probably even Maylee were judging me, thinking how strange I was, thinking I didn't understand basic social rules, like how *of course* you bring a tent when you go camping. They were thinking I was exactly like the stereotypes at Sunny Acres who are always waiting for handouts, waiting for someone else to figure out life for them.

PETRA

I mean, what else was I going to do? The girl needed a place to sleep. I didn't want to make it a bigger deal than it was, so I grabbed her sleeping bag and said, "I'll throw this in my tent, cool?"

Abigail nodded.

And that was that.

But seriously. Who goes camping without a tent?

9

You're doing great. We're going to take a
quick break now, check in with the others. Is
there anything we can get you in the meantime?

PETRA

Um...yeah? Maybe you could rescue my best friend from
the woods?

NOLAN

Any chance I could get some ibuprofen? I've got a killer
headache.

PETRA

And maybe answer some questions. Like is SAR on the scene?
Are you using drones? Have you brought in canines? Have
the others told you anything remotely logical, or are they still
repeating the same nonsense from this morning?

JOHN

I'm fine. Thank you for asking.

ABIGAIL

Could you try to call my dad again? He usually works long hours when he has an out-of-town job, but maybe he'll check his messages on a break.

PETRA

I suppose you could also get me another cup of coffee. Or rather this liquid you're calling coffee. It's sort of amazing how you've managed to make it both bitter and flavorless at the same time.

Oh, and by the way, apparently you haven't gotten this memo, but Styrofoam is bad for the environment.

But whatever. I've been up all night. I need the caffeine.

10

Let's get back to it. At that point in the trip, were there any strange occurrences?

PETRA
No.

ABIGAIL
I don't think so.

[pause]

Except... Actually, no. I don't know.

NOLAN
Has anyone mentioned the footprint?

ABIGAIL
It wasn't really *strange*. That's why I didn't bring it up right away.

It's not because I was trying to hide anything, I just...I don't know. It was only a footprint.

NOLAN

I've got pictures of it. Do you want to see?

PETRA

God, the *footprint*.

Do I really have to get into this?

[pause]

Fine.

After we set up camp, I asked everyone if they wanted to walk down to the creek before we lost daylight.

JOHN

I didn't want to hike to the creek. What's the appeal of walking through a forest where every tree looks the same? Now wandering a city, *that's* interesting.

[pause]

It's weird—before the camping trip, I thought Maylee felt the same.

PETRA

Everyone said yes, they wanted to go. Only before we started walking, John was like—

JOHN

I asked if it was okay to leave all our stuff at the campsite.

PETRA

I said, "John, what do you think's going to happen to it?"

As if some criminal might spend hours driving backcountry roads, hoping they'd stumble onto an untended campsite that *happened* to have some valuables.

Seriously, it only takes five minutes of talking to someone to figure out they're not used to being in nature.

JOHN

I generally don't drop my belongings somewhere and leave them unattended, right?

PETRA

So I convinced John it was fine, and we were all ready to go, when Nolan pulled out this little rectangular black box and clipped it to his phone. I asked him what it was. And you know what he told me?

NOLAN

It's a device that'll turn my phone into a thermal imager.

PETRA

Before we'd left the house, I got a peek at what Nolan packed in his duffel bag. He didn't bring food. He didn't bring sunscreen or hiking boots or cooking utensils. He basically didn't pack a single practical item for the trip. But he brought some thermal imaging crap?

NOLAN

Petra's glaring at me, and I'm thinking, "What? What can you possibly be mad at right now?" But before we can fight it out, Abigail says, "What's a thermal imager?"

So while the five of us walk from the campsite down to the water, Abigail and I hang in the back, and I tell her how the thermal imaging camera works and what it's used for.

PETRA

Abigail looked like she wanted to throw herself into the creek.

ABIGAIL

I didn't understand everything Nolan said, not exactly. But basically, he'd made it so his phone camera could see temperature.

He told me about how cops use thermal imaging sometimes if they're tracking someone in the dark—they can find a suspect just from their body heat. Or firefighters might use it to find the source of a fire, or maybe even to locate a person lost in smoke.

Nolan held up his phone so I could see the image. It was all tie-dye splashes of color. The trees in front of us were shades of blue, but Maylee and John were on-screen, too, walking ahead of us holding hands, and their skin showed in flaming reds and oranges.

I said, "Gosh, that's really interesting."

The only thing I didn't quite get was why he'd brought the thermal image thingy on the camping trip.

PETRA

I was in the lead, Maylee and John right behind me. The hill was steep and slippery with fallen leaves and pine needles, damp from recent rain. We weren't on a real trail, just a place where the foxglove and salmonberry bushes were sparse enough to let us pass—a game trail, maybe. I'd nearly reached the bottom when I heard Nolan shout, "Hey, wait!"

I waited.

And *waited*.

He said, "Come here, you've gotta see this."

I looked back and saw him crouched at the top of the hill,

staring at something on the ground. I called, "Nolan, if I walk all the way back up there, whatever you're looking at better be worth it."

He didn't respond. He'd started taking pictures.

NOLAN

It's a footprint. A nearly perfect impression in a patch of mud. The shape suggests something humanoid—except I know it wasn't made by a human because it's nearly double the length and width of my own foot.

I wear size ten, by the way. So just in case you're thinking the footprint only looks massive because I've got tiny feet, yeah, that's not what's going on.

PETRA

When I got to the top of the hill, Nolan said, "Look. It's a footprint. A *footprint*."

I glanced at it and said, "Yeah, except actually it's not."

He said, "Right here, this is the ball of the foot. And these are the toes."

It could have been anything, okay? I guess it *could* have been a footprint, but one of us could have made it if we shifted our feet a little when stepping. An animal could have made it when they took off running. A rock could have rolled by and hollowed out a soft patch of dirt. It wasn't a footprint. It was a freaking depression in the ground.

I told Nolan he was making a fool of himself. I told him that he wanted to believe his stupid cryptid narrative so badly that he was willing to twist reality to fit it.

He gave me this wounded look, and I was like, "Sorry if that upsets you, but I'm just telling it as it is."

NOLAN

Petra likes to say she [air quotes] tells it as it is.

And I'm always like, you know, that's just another way of saying you're an asshole.

PETRA

Why are you looking at me like that? You think I was being a jerk? I'm sorry, but can we back up a minute? You realize Nolan was looking for Bigfoot, right?

Bigfoot.

Go ahead and take a second to process that.

NOLAN

For the record, you should say *a* bigfoot.

If you claim someone "spotted Bigfoot," you're acting like Bigfoot is the creature's *name*. You'd say someone got "attacked by *a* lion," not "attacked by Lion," right? You wouldn't say "I saw Bear and Monkey at the zoo."

Bigfoots are a currently unknown bipedal mammal that got stuck with a ridiculous name in 1958 when the first footprints were publicized. And it sucks because it basically guarantees that people won't treat them as a legit species.

But yeah, at the very least, you can work on getting the terminology right.

JOHN

I'll back Nolan up on the footprint. It wasn't made by a cryptid, but it was definitely real.

[pause]

The size? I didn't measure it, but I guess a little bigger than my feet? I wear a twelve. Though it's hard to do an exact comparison, since whoever made the footprint wasn't wearing shoes.

ABIGAIL

Yes, there was a footprint.

I didn't see it at first—it just looked like a section of dirt that was kinda messed up? But once Nolan pointed it out, I was like, okay, I guess that's a footprint.

John thought so, too. He said, "Anyone else find it concerning that someone is wandering around the woods *barefoot*?"

PETRA

Maylee shivered and said, "Okay, that's really creepy. You don't think..." Then she looked around quickly, as if she was scared someone might be lurking in the trees.

I was like, *seriously*?

Then she caught my eye and winked.

NOLAN

The truth is, maybe I didn't *really* think I was gonna find evidence of a cryptid species at Salvation Creek. Maybe I figured I'd report back to NACRO that I tried but no luck, better stick to places with more consistent sightings, more mysterious disappearances.

But now I'm looking at this print and not only is it evidence of a large humanoid creature, I find it thirty minutes after getting to the campsite.

Incredible, right?

Something like that happens, you almost have to think it's fate.

I take some pictures—regular, not thermal—and jot down notes. Wish I had plaster or something to make a cast of it, not that I have a clue how to do that.

I try to remember when it last rained.

Two, three nights ago?

That means the footprint is recent. And it occurs to me that a footprint that fresh, just a couple yards from our campsite...

JOHN

That was when I first suspected we weren't alone at Salvation Creek.

It could've been my mind playing tricks on me. But right then, it really felt like we were being watched.

11

What can you tell us about John Massey? Do you think it's possible he'd hurt Maylee?

NOLAN

I hardly know John. We see each other around, but I wouldn't call him a *friend*.

I also wouldn't call him the kind of guy who'd hurt his girlfriend.

PETRA

Do I think John...

[laughs]

Are you kidding me?

No. I do *not* think John could have hurt Maylee. That might rank as the single most absurd thing I've ever heard.

NOLAN

The worst I can say about John is that he comes off as fake. Like, even though we're hardly even acquaintances, whenever I see him, he gives me this big grin and is all, "What's new, Nolan? How's life treating you? Watch any good shows lately?"

Come on. No one is legitimately *that* friendly.

It's like he never got the memo that after being elected student council VP, he could stop campaigning.

PETRA

Honestly, John might be the nicest person I know. He makes friends with *everyone*. I don't just mean at school but, like, with the clerk at the grocery store or receptionist at the dentist's office or a random person walking down the street. I've never seen anyone start conversations so easily.

ABIGAIL

John was really nice yesterday, which I guess kinda surprised me. In the car, on the way to the campsite, he noticed my charm bracelet and was asking all about it.

[holds out wrist]

See? On every birthday, my dad gets me a charm to repre-sent something important that happened that year. The musical note is from my fourteenth birthday because I joined church choir. The rifle is from my tenth birthday because that's when my dad started taking me hunting. And see, this one looks like a tiny driver's license—from when I turned sixteen, of course.

Anyhow, John was asking about the meaning behind the charms, and he seemed to really care, you know? Lots of times people ask you questions, but as soon as you answer, it's like they stop listening. Not John. He made me feel like he was super interested in everything I had to say.

He was so nice that…I guess I started to wonder if the rumors about him were wrong.

PETRA
What?

[pause]

I mean, yeah? I don't know how I could have been clearer. John is super outgoing and talkative.

[pause]

Oh, really, he hasn't been forthcoming with *you*? Gee. Do you think it's because he's been treated like a criminal since we got here?

NOLAN

As for John and Maylee's relationship, I couldn't tell you much about it. Seems to me that the only thing they had in common was being popular. Maybe that was enough for them. Or maybe they were actually soul mates or some bullshit. How should I know?

[pause]

You wanna hear something curious, though? They started dating right after the accident. I'm talking within a *week*. You've gotta figure John was in a really screwed-up mental place—and Maylee knew it. Would they have gotten together if he'd been thinking clearly?

I'm just saying, it seems like a lot of Maylee's relationships have extenuating circumstances.

ABIGAIL

Maylee and John had been dating for...about a year, I guess? A little longer? Yesterday was the first time I saw them interact, though.

Well, I guess I should say it's the first time I saw them interact from *up close*. Because of course I saw them together at school. Not that I was specifically watching or anything, because why would I do that? But I'd pass them in the halls and stuff, so technically I *did* see them together.

Huh?

Oh, right. Yes, on the camping trip Maylee and John seemed happy.

They seemed in love.

[pause]

Did you ask Petra and Nolan this question, too?

PETRA

You'll probably think I'm trash for saying this, but I've always thought John was too nice for Maylee.

It's like this: You can't let your guard down around him. Like, maybe I want to complain about Mr. Meyers—that's our World History teacher—and say he gives me total serial killer vibes. John would jump in and be like, "I agree Mr. Meyers is a weird dude, but it's not cool to joke like that. Someone might overhear and get the wrong idea."

Obviously he'd be right, and I'd know it. But sometimes, when I'm having a crap day, I just need to vent and, I don't know, say ugly things.

And Maylee, she's like me. She needs space to be ugly. When she's feeling angry or bitter or jealous or whatever, she lets it out. Except when John's around. It always surprised me that she could censor that part of herself around him.

But they've been dating for a year, and somehow she's making it work. So what do I know?

ABIGAIL

Thinking about it now, I feel kinda...I don't know. Ashamed, maybe? All John had to do was show the slightest bit of interest in my life, and just like that, I forgot all my reservations about him.

Nana Abbie says I'm an innocent soul, but what she really means is that I'm gullible. She says I have to be careful people don't take advantage of me. I guess maybe she's right.

Because no matter how nice and attentive John might have been, the night ended in him—

[pause]

Could I have a some more tissues?

[pause]

Thank you.

I'm sorry.

I just still can't believe Maylee is dead.

PETRA

Did John request a lawyer?

He's smart; I bet he did.

Though that probably only makes you more suspicious of him, doesn't it? You know what's unfair? We have this whole system to give people who are accused of crimes the means to protect themselves. Yet as soon as someone actually takes advantage of those means—like by getting a lawyer—they immediately look guilty.

[pause]

Look, I understand why you need to ask these questions. When a woman goes missing, her significant other is most often to blame. I *get* that. But is that what's happening here? Are you suspicious of John because he's Maylee's boyfriend? Or, let's be real, is this actually about him being Black?

12

Let's focus on the sequence of events again.
After you found the footprint, you went
down to the creek. What did you do there?

PETRA

Okay, first of all it wasn't a footprint, so you can stop calling it that.

But anyway, after that little incident, we started trekking down the hill again. Nolan and Abigail were a few steps behind me, and he kept babbling nonstop about Bigfoot crap. Abigail was like, "Oh...um, okay. That's interesting..."

Maylee and I glanced at each other and tried not to laugh. John must have noticed us because he was like, "Hey, I actually find it pretty interesting, too."

I heard Nolan tell Abigail, "Awareness of bigfoots really exploded in 1967. That's when one of them was documented for the first time. The Patterson–Gimlin film shows an apelike creature walking through the—"

Abigail interrupted Nolan, probably because she'd do anything to get him to shut up. She was like, "Oh yeah, I think I've seen that footage."

Of course, it didn't even register to Nolan that he was being shut down. He said, and this is beyond embarrassing, he said, "Maybe you'd be interested in this little piece of trivia: The bigfoot in the film is actually a female. People call her Patty."

At that point, I just wanted the Bigfoot conversation to end. Nolan's interests are his own business, and if he wants to dedicate his life to an imaginary creature, whatever. But that doesn't mean *I* should have to hear about it.

But instead of doing me a favor and changing topics, Maylee gave me this sly smile and said, "Hey, Nolan, how'd anyone know Bigfoot was a girl? Was she wearing makeup? Do bigfeet conform to gender stereotypes?"

That's when Nolan should've stopped talking. But of course he can't let anything go. He got the superior tone he uses whenever he's being challenged and said, "It's clear the bigfoot in the video is female because she has breasts."

And I was like, "Oh my God, Nolan, you are *not* talking about Bigfoot's *breasts*."

Maylee laughed so hard that I thought she might tumble all the way down the hill and into the creek.

JOHN

I didn't like the way everyone was laughing at Nolan, so I pulled Maylee aside and told her to go a little easier on him. She started getting defensive and I told her, "I know you're just playing around, but it comes off as harsh sometimes."

She seemed to understand.

NOLAN

Maylee making fun of me wasn't exactly new. Mockery was basically her primary means of communication.

[pause]

No. I wouldn't say it *bothered* me. That would imply I actually found value in her opinion.

I get that we're not supposed to talk bad about the dead. But if you ask around, you'll find this out anyway: I don't like Maylee. She's the most selfish, manipulative person I've ever met. You think I'm exaggerating? Ask Ray about her when he gets back to the station. Because I've overheard him lecturing Petra about [air quotes] recognizing unhealthy relationships, and I'm pretty sure he wasn't talking in the abstract.

I'm not saying I'm glad Maylee's dead or anything. But yeah, I won't pretend I'll miss her.

ABIGAIL

When we got to the creek, Nolan stopped talking, which was kinda disappointing. I'm not super into bigfoots or anything, but isn't it always great to have a conversation with someone on a subject they're super passionate about? Even Maylee was interested and asking him questions.

But anyhow, at the bottom of the hill, he dropped the conversation. We were all quiet for a second, taking in the view. Salvation Creek isn't very wide, but it runs fast, and the water sparkles on sunny days. Pretty close to where we were standing, there was this huge boulder jutting out over the deepest part of the creek.

PETRA

Of course Maylee had to immediately climb to the top of the boulder, which basically gave me heart failure. She was wearing this pair of flimsy canvas slip-ons, which isn't exactly ideal for rock scrambling.

I was thinking, what happens if she slips? What happens if she breaks a leg? We're *hours* from civilization.

Clearly, John was having those thoughts, too, because he joked, "I hope you don't think I'm carrying you to the car when you fall and sprain your ankle."

Maylee laughed and said, "You'd leave me stranded?"

John was like, "Nope, I'll make Petra carry you. She's stronger than me anyway."

He was smiling and trying to keep his tone all lighthearted, but yeah, I could tell Maylee was making him nervous.

JOHN

Maylee was ten feet up on a rock, bouncing around like she was invincible. Of course I was nervous.

NOLAN

Salvation Creek has all these boulders around it. Granite, you know? The thing is, granite is one of the location commonalties. Whether we're talking Yosemite, the Smoky Mountains, basically anywhere with clusters of mysterious disappearances, there's always large quantities of granite.

PETRA

Nolan said...what?

[pause]

Sorry, I'm just trying to figure out what the crap granite could possibly have to do with disappearances.

NOLAN

I'm not saying it *means* anything. I'm just breaking down some statistics.

There are certain heavily forested areas of North America that have a disproportionately large number of mysterious disappearances.

These locations often have commonalities, like being near granite.

These locations also happen to be among the areas where bigfoot sightings are most frequently reported.

Those are *facts*. Analyze them how you will.

JOHN

Maylee asked me to take her photo—she's always asking me to take photos of her. I'm sure that would get old for some people, but I like making her happy. Plus, I've learned a decent amount about photography in the past year.

ABIGAIL

Maylee has this huge social media following. Huge compared to me, at least. But I guess most people have more followers than me, because I only post like once a month, usually when I find a quote in a book that's so great I just have to share it.

But anyhow, *thousands* of people follow Maylee.

I always thought it must feel weird to know that strangers are peeking into your life. Like, I'd see the comments on Maylee's photos, and all these people she didn't know would be referencing her favorite breakfast spot or the shoes she'd worn a few days before or what show she was bingeing.

If I were in that position, I'd feel like my life belonged to other people more than it belonged to me. But that's just a personality thing, I guess, because Maylee loved all the attention. She used to say, "What's even the point of doing anything if no one's watching?"

NOLAN

Some of the other commonalities:

People disappearing while berry-picking.

People disappearing and leaving behind an essential item, like a cell phone.

People disappearing right before sudden changes in weather.

This is why we need organizations like NACRO, see? All these little commonalities seem meaningless alone, but they must add up to something.

PETRA

I told Maylee to get off the boulder before she slipped and broke her freaking neck. She gave me a wicked smile, then turned and stepped closer to the edge. One more foot forward and she'd be plunging into Salvation Creek.

I said, "Seriously, Maylee, not cool."

She called back, "There's no rocks below me. I could probably jump in."

And I was like, "Um, yeah, and get hypothermia."

I mean, the weather was nice enough, but the creek water flows down from the mountains. It's frigid. And cold water can cause hypothermia in like seventy-degree weather.

But when has Maylee ever listened to me? Instead of getting down, she spread her arms out like she was going to either dive in or take flight.

JOHN

I took some photos of Maylee standing at the edge of the boulder with her arms spread wide. From where I stood, the creek below her wasn't visible. She could have stepped off the edge into anything.

I knew Maylee would like them. Her favorite pictures of herself are the ones where she pretends she's not posing.

ABIGAIL

When Maylee finally climbed down from the boulder, she held out her hand to John. He passed her his phone, and she went through the pictures. She said, "I'm favoriting the ones I want you to send me when we have service again, okay? These are going to get a lot of likes."

PETRA

Ah yes, Maylee's influencer career...

[sighs]

Look...she's very passionate about it. And of course I'm going to support anything my best friend is passionate about, even if it's not my thing.

Once I told her, "You know everything on social media is fake, right?"

Maylee was like, "Duh, Petra, that's the whole point. Who wants to live in the real world?"

NOLAN

Do I think Maylee was gonna, what, be a famous influencer?

[snorts]

She has like five thousand followers. I doubt brands were knocking down her door with sponsorships.

PETRA

Isn't there a more important conversation we could be having right now? Or even better, I could be, you know, helping you actually *search for Maylee*. I just don't see the benefit of sitting here chatting about her career prospects.

[pause]

Here's the truth: Maylee's socials look good. They're pretty, she's pretty, the pictures and videos are pretty. But there are thousands of pretty accounts out there.

When I asked if she had a backup plan, in case being an influencer didn't work out, do you know what she said to me? She said, "Making backup plans is for people who don't believe in themselves."

I wanted to help her—obviously, I don't want to see my best friend fail—so I tried explaining that she needs a niche. Something that sets her apart from all the other people trying to do the exact same thing. Like, there are fashion influencers and gamer influencers and fitness influencers. She didn't want to hear it, though.

Maylee is more of a concept person. She has great ideas, but when it comes to turning those details into an actual plan...let's just say she loses focus real quick.

NOLAN

The only reason she has *any* followers is because she's hot, okay?

JOHN

Maylee's career didn't take off the way she'd hoped. She worried about that a lot. I always told her the same thing: She was fairly new to being an influencer, and these things took time. I made sure she knew I believed in her, though. That I was sure she'd be successful.

[pause]

But I also reminded her that college was still an option.

PETRA

So Maylee shinnied off the boulder, talking about our camping trip in terms of followers and likes. And she said something about how she'll get a mini travel post out of it, which will be great practice for next year.

I was thinking, what happens next year?

Before I could ask, Abigail said something like, "Are you still planning on Mykonos first?"

Mykonos?

First?

I stood there like, what the crap is this girl talking about?

I waited for Maylee to have a similar response. Instead, she looked at Abigail and flippantly said, "Probably. But I'm not really setting anything in stone. Que sera sera."

I asked if someone would please tell me what was going on. Maylee gave me this innocent look, extra-wide brown eyes. She said, "I'm planning to put college on hold for a year or two. Spend some time traveling and building my brand. You know that."

Um, pardon me?

I did *not* know that.

Maylee said, "I must have mentioned it a million times."

I was like, "Traveling *where*?"

She shrugged and said, "I don't know. Everywhere."

I asked for how long.

She told me she didn't know that, either.

I said, "How exactly are you funding this?" I mean, Maylee's mom is an orthodontist, so they're not exactly hurting for money. But her mom has also made it clear that as much as she loves Maylee, she does *not* support the whole influencer dream.

Maylee only sighed, as if *I* was being difficult, and said, "I don't have every little detail planned out, okay, Petra? Why are you making this into some big thing? You must have known this was always the end goal."

I knew she wanted to be an influencer, yeah. But I didn't know she was actively taking steps toward making it happen. And that *did* feel like a big thing to me. I'm not sure if I can explain this exactly right, but...I guess it felt like there was suddenly a huge area of Maylee's life that I wasn't part of.

Just to compare, the night before the camping trip, after I'd gone over my checklist one last time, I called Maylee. I told her what my family had eaten for dinner and what show I was putting on TV and debated whether I should add another pair of socks to my backpack. I told her every pointless detail of my life, and she couldn't even tell me a *huge* thing like she was planning on traveling the world next year instead of starting college with me?

You can see why I was feeling a little weird, right?

Anyway, I wasn't going to say all that while Nolan and John and Abigail were around—especially when John was already giving me this sympathetic look. So instead, I just said, "Okay, then. Cool. Good luck with that."

[pause]

No, I'm not *angry* about it. I was just a little hurt, okay? I was standing there at Salvation Creek, during a camping trip that was already going wrong, wondering why *Abigail Buckley* somehow knew more about my best friend's life than I did.

JOHN

I hadn't known Maylee was making specific plans for next year. We don't talk much about the future.

[pause]

Why?

Because what we want from life isn't exactly compatible. What good would it do, constantly being reminded that our relationship has an expiration date?

[pause]

But yes, I did find it odd that Maylee had discussed her plans with Abigail.

NOLAN

Maylee totally blindsided Petra. She's trying to act all tough but doing the thing where she talks really fast to hide that she's on the verge of tears. I want to tell her not to take the situation so seriously because I doubt anything will come of it. I'd heard Maylee announce other grand plans over the years, and can you guess how often she follows through?

Eventually, Maylee tells Petra, "We'll talk about this later, okay?" Then she walks away and starts wandering along the creek. Abigail follows with this serious expression and whispers something to her.

[pause]

No, I didn't hear what she said—but I wasn't exactly trying to. Sorry, but whatever drama they had going on didn't interest me.

ABIGAIL

Petra was so weird when I mentioned Maylee going to Mykonos next year. Her voice changed and she started talking in this curt way. It made me feel like I'd said something wrong, but I couldn't figure out what.

Because Petra *must* have known about Maylee's plans, right? Everyone at school knew she was trying to be an influencer.

[pause]

When did *I* find out about it?

[pause]

I guess it must have been...maybe the end of sophomore year? So like a year and a half ago. I remember being with Maylee at this park near Sunny Acres. We were wandering around, and I was noticing for the first time how brown the grass was and how rickety the playground equipment looked. I wished I'd suggested somewhere nicer to go. Maylee never minded about stuff like that, though.

I don't know how the topic came up, but at one point, Maylee said, "Have you ever thought about modeling? If I had your body, I would've signed with an agency ages ago."

The thing is, it actually really annoys me when people say I should be a model just because I'm tall and skinny. It almost annoys me as much as when people make jokes and call me stuff like "praying mantis." Why does anyone think it's okay to comment on someone else's body? But all I said to Maylee was that I didn't like getting my picture taken and I'd *hate* being famous.

She rolled her eyes like I was messing around and said, "Come on. You wouldn't hate it."

I told her that I really, really would.

And she said, "I don't believe you. No one wants to be insignificant."

It took me a second to even understand what she was saying because, I don't know, I just never thought of fame and significance as the same thing?

Anyhow, that was when she told me all about her dreams of being an influencer. She talked about the clothes she'd wear and the places she'd travel and how, wherever she went, people would watch her.

I asked her if she could really live like that, with the world scrutinizing her every move. Like, if you're famous, you get all these people telling you how great you are all the time...but there's this whole other group of people who watch you just for excuses to tear you down.

Maylee said, "Honestly, I don't care if people love me or hate me. The worst thing would be if no one thought of me at all."

I already knew *that* wouldn't be a problem. Maylee lit up every room she walked into. You probably think I'm exaggerating. But ask anyone; I swear they'll tell you the same thing. Maylee was special.

She really could have been a famous influencer.

She could have been anything if she had the chance.

13

Petra, it looks like there's
something you want to say.

PETRA

Oh wow, what truly excellent detective work.

There's *a lot* I freaking want to say. Like, why haven't you found Maylee? Why aren't you giving me updates? Do you honestly think one of us is hiding something?

[pause]

Or maybe you think we're *all* hiding something together? I bet that's on your list of theories, isn't it? That we're *conspiring*. For the record, that's completely illogical. It's been forever since you were in high school, so maybe your memory is foggy, but it's pretty much impossible for *one* person to keep a secret. There's zero chance of four of us doing it.

[long pause]

FYI, I realize that when you sit there for a long time without speaking, it's a tactic. Most people hate silence so much that they'll start talking just to fill it. My brother is the worst about that—as you've probably noticed. Every time Nolan gets nervous, he starts rattling off facts. God forbid he be given a polygraph. He'd probably get so worked up that he'd fail the control questions.

[pause]

You're not actually going to make us take lie detector tests though, are you? There's a reason those aren't admissible in court.

Though, according to my dad, eyewitness testimony isn't much better. He says it's the worst sort of evidence because people see what they want to see. They miss details and let their brains fill in the gaps. Eventually, it's impossible to distinguish between real memories or invented ones.

The problem isn't that witnesses lie to the police. It's that they lie to *themselves*.

Anyway. I'm telling you crap you should've already learned during your career. But I would've also expected you to learn when to cut an interview short because a witness's skills could be better used elsewhere.

So yeah.

Who knows?

14

So you spend some time down by the creek.
Then what? You go back up to the campsite?

PETRA

That's what I *wanted* to do. I told everyone we should head back and get a fire going. John said that was a good idea because he was hungry, and we started up the hill. Nolan was in the back, absorbed by his stupid thermal image thing. Suddenly, he shouted.

NOLAN

Petra's complaining about being hungry. She starts heading toward the campsite, but the rest of us aren't so eager to get back. I'd hardly gotten a chance to use my thermal imager, so I hold it up, point it farther down the creek where the trees are denser and have all these vines winding up them.

   And that's when I see it:

A flash of red on the screen.

ABIGAIL

Red meant heat.

Red meant something was in the woods ahead of us. Something alive.

NOLAN

It's only a blur, then the forest returns to its cool-temperature blues and greens. But I know something—a mammal—is out here. And from my brief glimpse, I think it's a hominid.

Maylee grabs on to John's arm like she's scared and says, "You don't think it's whoever made the footprint, do you?"

Petra starts to respond, but I ask everyone to be quiet.

PETRA

I told Nolan to please not *shush* me.

God, he was all worked up. He kept saying he'd seen something on his thermal imager. Some sort of animal. I looked where he was pointing but didn't see anything—not that I *would* have. The vegetation in that section of woods is so thick it's a wall in some places.

I was like, "We're in the forest, Nolan. Have you not heard of *deer*?"

JOHN

Petra said Nolan probably saw a deer, right? Thing is, that didn't make me feel any safer. Bambi might look friendly, but I'm guessing his antlers could cause serious damage.

NOLAN

When you're in a situation like this, basically the worst thing you can do is barrel ahead without a plan. And I don't have one.

But I decide that's a problem for future me. I'm so pumped that everything I learned through NACRO about taking precautions flies out of my head. I start moving forward through the woods. I start following whatever I'd seen.

ABIGAIL

I was kinda engrossed in my conversation with Maylee right then. Part of my brain heard everything Nolan said and realized he was chasing something deeper into the woods, but it also *didn't* register at the same time.

If I'd been paying more attention, I would've tried to stop him.

JOHN

Next thing I knew, everyone was following Nolan deeper into the forest. What was I going to do, stand there alone?

PETRA

Last year my dad let me take this survival training class, the same one people take when they're joining a SAR team. He said it's good to learn the skills, even if I'm too young to join searches.

The thing my instructor pounded into our heads is that you never know when you're entering a survival situation.

It's not like a movie, where the soundtrack becomes ominous as soon as you make a wrong turn. It's usually not even *one* wrong turn. When people get lost in the wilderness, it's because of a series of tiny mistakes that wouldn't have amounted to anything on their own.

You forget to pack a signal flare. You underestimate the terrain. You don't have the right jacket.

Maybe your map is outdated. Maybe you forgot to tell anyone where you're going. Maybe you just step down in a slightly wrong way and your ankle twists under you.

When someone gets lost in the woods, people always say, "Why didn't they just stay put? Haven't they heard of Hug-a-Tree?"

It's the first rule of the wilderness: Stay where you are and wait for someone to save you. If you're lost, you don't want to risk circling around SAR. You don't want to stumble into an area that's already been searched.

Easier said than done. Because, at the moment, the person

doesn't even realize they're in danger. They don't know how their series of small mistakes—mistakes they haven't even noticed—are piling up.

They don't know they've entered a survival situation.

NOLAN

The creature is on the other side of Salvation Creek. I follow along the shore until I get to a place where the water is shallow and littered with big rocks.

Behind me, John is like, "Hey, man, I know you really want to see what's out here, but maybe we should wait until we're more prepared."

I ignore him and duck under a low branch covered in dangling moss and go right up to the creek's edge.

Petra says, "Nolan, don't even think about it."

But I'm not thinking about it, I'm *doing* it. I'm jumping from rock to rock, weaving and wobbling. They're slippery as fuck, totally covered in algae, and yeah, okay, right about then it would've been nice to have something sturdy on my feet. Something with more grip and ankle support than Chucks. But I'm not exactly gonna stop what I'm doing and praise Petra for the foresight to wear hiking boots.

One, two, three big rocks.

Then I'm on the other side, cut off from everyone else by the creek. I don't dwell on it, don't even consider how alone I'll be if they don't follow me. Because right then, there's another flash of red on my camera.

PETRA

Nolan was being so freaking reckless. He was putting *all* of us in danger. Because of course I wasn't just going to watch him run headlong into the woods. I wasn't going to abandon my brother.

So I crossed the creek, too.

JOHN

The situation felt very chaotic. Everyone was running through the forest, Maylee nearly fell while trying to cross the creek, Nolan kept shouting about what he saw on his thermal camera. If he wanted to catch the creature so badly, maybe he should have kept his voice down.

ABIGAIL

I crossed the creek behind Maylee. That's when I started paying attention to where we were, exactly. And I...

[pause]

I don't know. I thought it was probably a bad idea to go that direction? So deep into the woods, I mean. The trees were thick, and the ground was covered in so many pine needles that you couldn't follow your footsteps back if you got lost. Plus, the air had that heavy, humid feeling, like a storm was coming. It just seemed like we should stay close to the campsite.

I tried telling everyone that, but I guess no one heard me.

Up ahead, Petra called after Nolan, saying we didn't have flashlights or extra water or jackets.

Nolan kinda slowed down, like maybe he was listening to her. It gave the rest of us a chance to catch up.

Petra said, "You don't know what you're following, Nolan. It could be a freaking cougar. It could be a *bear*."

Nolan said it wasn't a bear.

Petra told him he didn't *know* that and how even if we had the right equipment, chasing a random animal is super dangerous.

Maylee said, "Petra is right."

PETRA

I just about fell over when Maylee agreed with me. Since when was she the voice of reason? I expected her to try chasing down Nolan's animal so she could get a picture with it. I can't even imagine how many likes a grizzly bear would get.

NOLAN

I hear them.

I hear every word they're saying.

But all I can think is, "This is it. This is it." A branch catches my hair, but I hardly feel it. My foot comes down hard on a pine cone, my ankle rolls, but I don't even slow down.

I look down at the thermal imager again, and...there's nothing but blues and greens. Cool temperatures. I wait. I point it at another section of the forest.

But the bigfoot is gone.

ABIGAIL

Nolan looked down at his phone, and it was like his whole face cracked open from sadness.

Petra asked him what was wrong, and he said, "The creature is gone."

I was relieved because I didn't want to keep going that way. But I was sad for Nolan, too. Looking at his face, seeing him realize he wasn't going to find what he was searching for, it was like how Maylee might look if she found out she'd never be famous.

PETRA

I told Nolan it was time to head back. I grabbed him by the elbow and started to lead him toward the creek, but he pulled away and said, "Just a little farther."

I opened my mouth to argue, but then shut it again. What

would it really matter if we went another couple yards into the forest? No, it wasn't exactly safe. And no, we weren't actually following some Bigfoot creature or whatever. But...

Oh God, it's so sappy to say, but I started thinking about when Nolan and I were kids and this Bigfoot stuff started. That was a really rough time for him. And, like, Nolan's feelings were real even if what he was chasing wasn't. I guess I felt bad for him. I wanted to give him a few more minutes of hope or something.

I pulled out my compass and checked our direction—I'd give in to him for a second, but I was *not* going to risk us getting turned around. I said, "Two more minutes, then we go back. I'm setting a timer."

JOHN

I wasn't thrilled with Petra unilaterally making decisions for the group. But before I could voice my opinion, she'd set her phone timer, and Nolan was walking deeper into the woods.

PETRA

Dusk was approaching, and we were far from the campsite in a section of old-growth forest where lichen crept up Douglas firs and jungly, oversized ferns brushed our arms—and we were there pursuing a freaking cryptid. Not exactly my finest moment, okay?

Nolan was at the front of the group, frantically pointing his camera into the brush, hoping for another glimpse of his creature. Maylee and Abigail were behind me, and they were...

[pause]

Okay.

[pause]

So I was feeling a little sensitive, all right? Because of the whole thing about Maylee traveling next year and Abigail apparently knowing before me. Anyway, it was probably just because I was already on edge, but it felt like...like Maylee and Abigail were purposefully keeping distance from me.

They were whispering to each other, and I turned around and asked what they were talking about. They both looked guilty.

Maylee said, "What? We're not talking about anything."

Which was obviously a lie.

So I was just like, fine, you don't want to tell me, forget it. I went and walked next to John, who was the only one not frustrating me.

[pause]

Well, no, everything wasn't *really* fine. I was having all these worries, like were Maylee and I not actually that close? What else hadn't she told me about? Was I really as much her friend as she was mine?

I was so distracted by my own thoughts that it took me a second to notice that the forest was getting easier to walk through. The thick vegetation had cleared out.

We'd ended up on a trail.

NOLAN

Petra calls ahead to me that we're on a trail.

And I'm like, yeah, no kidding. That's why I'm able to move so much faster now. I tell her, "Let's go a little farther. I want to see what's at the end of it."

She says, "Oh my God, it's going to lead to a scenic overlook or something, Nolan. It's a *hiking trail*."

But I have a feeling she's wrong. That's why, when her two-minute timer beeps, I keep walking.

ABIGAIL

Petra said Maylee and I were being weird?

[pause]

No, I don't know why she would have thought that.

PETRA

Nolan hurried through the woods, and I followed after him, calling, "What, you think Bigfoot made this trail? You think it's leading us to his house?"

Except I guess the joke was on me.

Because we ended up at a cabin.

NOLAN

Well, sure, I'm disappointed.

I was kind of expecting to see a different type of shelter at the end of the trail. It's another one of those commonalities. In cluster areas, places with lots of unexplained disappearances, search parties regularly find crude structures made of branches and sticks.

I'm not saying the structures were made by bigfoots, just like I'm not saying that bigfoots are definitely abducting girls from Salvation Creek. I'm just laying out the facts. It's a *fact* that people disappear in the woods, and it's a *fact* that these makeshift huts are often found nearby. It's a fact that some people at NACRO have linked that with bigfoot sightings. Draw your own conclusions.

So anyway, when I'm running down the trail, I get it in my head that one of those shelters—some people at NACRO actually think they're nests—is gonna be at the end. In fact, I'm *sure* of it.

I'm not getting any more hits with my thermal imager, but I do notice a bunch of broken tree branches. I call that info back to the group, and Petra's like, "What the crap does that even mean? Why would Bigfoot randomly go around breaking branches?"

I see a gouge on a tree trunk, and I know it could be claw marks. I should stop and take pictures, but I can't slow down; it feels like there's too much at stake. It feels like I'm *so close*.

So yeah. When we burst into the clearing and see a regular cabin, I'm pretty disheartened.

JOHN

It's too generous to call it a cabin. It was a shack.

PETRA

Nolan had the smuggest look on his face. I was sure he was thinking, "See, Petra? I knew the trail would lead to *something*."

Fine, he was right. But excuse me for assuming that an area full of hiking trails would put us *on a hiking trail*. Whatever.

I was like, "Okay, you proved a point. There's a cabin. Can we please go back to the campsite now?"

John said, "I second that idea."

NOLAN

I'm standing there feeling like a huge idiot. I led everyone into the woods for nothing. I'd been so sure there was a bigfoot ahead of us. Or at least *evidence* of one. And instead we're at some completely ordinary cabin.

But then I think, how do I *know* it's ordinary? Like, I realize bigfoots don't build houses, but that doesn't mean one hadn't been inside after it was abandoned and maybe, I don't know, left evidence behind. So I say, "Since we're here anyway, why don't we check the cabin out?"

PETRA

Um, pardon me?

Why don't we check out the cabin?

Probably because it freaking *belongs* to someone, and I'm not turning our camping trip into criminal trespassing. John was nodding as I spoke and I was glad there was at least one other law-abiding person on the camping trip.

But then he said—

ABIGAIL

"I don't need any trouble with the police."

Petra crossed her arms and was like, "Not all cops are bad, you know."

There was a silence, then John said, "Okay."

But it definitely wasn't *really* okay. And Petra started saying her dad was a good guy and that he'd done a lot to help John out last year. John sort of laughed—but an upset laugh, like he couldn't even believe her—and was like, "You really want to get into this right now?"

So yeah, it was super awkward.

JOHN

I'm sorry, but I won't sit here and pretend I've had great experiences with law enforcement.

PETRA

I hadn't meant to start anything—I just get defensive when I think someone is insulting my dad. I told John I was sorry and we moved on.

[pause]

Don't look at me like that. I know how to apologize, okay?

Anyway. The conversation didn't go any further, because Nolan pointed at the cabin and said, "Come on, Petra, you can't possibly think someone *lives* here."

I tried explaining that no one had ever *lived* in the cabin. It was for hunting—probably only used on weekends in fall—not someone's permanent residence. I told him it might look abandoned, but it almost certainly wasn't, and we had no right to barge in.

JOHN

The shack was hardly standing. The wood was water-damaged and full of gaps; no insulation at all. The windows were so grimy you couldn't see through them. There was a chimney, not brick, but the kind from a woodstove, tilted at a forty-five-degree angle. The next good storm might blow the whole place over.

Legal issues aside, I didn't want to hang out there.

NOLAN

So I ask, "When's hunting season?"

Abigail and Maylee are hanging back, acting all weird and quiet. Abigail says, "It's deer season right now."

I point out that if hunting season is currently going on, then, in theory, the cabin should be in use. But it's not. The place is abandoned. It's so clearly abandoned—for decades, probably. Meaning it's cool for us to go inside.

Maylee scoots closer to John—who's shaking his head like going in the cabin is the worst idea he's ever heard—and gives him this big-eyed look. She's all, "It's just like that movie we watched the other night, isn't it?"

John says, "I sure hope not."

JOHN

The movie was a low-budget slasher called *Carnage Cabin*. Not something I would've chosen, especially right before a camping trip, but it had been Maylee's turn to pick.

[pause]

We didn't actually finish the movie. It got too bloody for me. Maylee cracked a joke about how my mom is a phlebotomist who spends all day drawing patients' blood, yet I can't even handle looking at a paper cut.

She's not wrong.

PETRA

Of course Maylee made John watch some in-the-woods horror movie before camping. I kid you not, the girl once put on a movie about a homicidal torture-dentist the night before she got her teeth cleaned.

ABIGAIL

I was about to tell Nolan that I agreed with the others: we should leave the cabin alone and go back to the campsite. But just then, he reached out and tried the door.

It was unlocked.

NOLAN

I step into the cabin's dim light. Behind me, Petra is ordering me to *get out right now*, and Maylee is asking John, "Wasn't that movie based on a true story?"

PETRA

I only followed Nolan inside so I could drag him out.

JOHN

What was it like in the shack?

[pause]

My lawyer advises me not to answer that question.

NOLAN

It's only one room. There's a woodstove in the left corner.

PETRA

A woodstove with fresh firewood piled near it.

NOLAN

There's a cot pushed under one window.

PETRA

A cot covered with a clean blanket.

NOLAN

A rickety little table and two mismatched chairs. The table has a misshapen purple vase on it that reminds me of elementary school art projects.

PETRA

There were faded curtains covering the windows. Two camping lanterns. A stack of battered paperbacks and a cabinet stocked with canned goods. A hunting jacket hung on a peg by the door—a camouflage monstrosity with more pockets than anyone could possibly need.

Look, I don't know anything about hunting, okay? My dad taught me to shoot for self-defense, but he says being a cop has made him distrust anyone who kills another creature for sport. But even with my limited knowledge, I could tell that jacket was expensive.

You get what I'm saying?

It wasn't the sort of thing someone would abandon.

NOLAN

Petra starts full-on freaking out. She's all, "We're breaking into someone's property right now. Do you realize that's a Class C misdemeanor?"

I glance back at Maylee and Abigail, and they're hovering in the doorway like they'll catch fire if they step through. Abigail's even paler than usual and her eyes look huge. John doesn't help. He's babbling nonstop, things like, "What's with these knives? Why would anyone need ten different knives? Seriously, does anyone else feel like we're being watched?"

Maylee says, "I've felt that way for a while now."

JOHN

I will say that yes, I expressed my discomfort with the shack.

PETRA

I mean, I wasn't overjoyed about the knives, either—it's pretty freaking sinister when you see a bunch of them displayed on a wall like that—but it's also what I'd *expect* to find in a hunting cabin.

John was seriously shaken, though, like he legit thought Leatherface might burst inside with a chainsaw. Maylee chose that moment to look toward the woods nervously and say, "Did anyone hear that? It sounded like footsteps."

I told her to cut it out. She flashed me a mischievous smile and went over to Abigail, who was still standing just outside the door. Maylee leaned in close and whispered something in her ear. Which, okay, *rude*. But whatever.

I turned to Nolan, and was like, "John's right; we need to get out of here."

John said, "*Thank you*, Petra."

For the record, it wasn't because I thought we were in some serial killer lair or something, but because—as I think I've said about a million times now—we were doing something *illegal*.

NOLAN

So yeah, I'm already sure there's nothing interesting in the cabin, but I'm ignoring Petra just to screw with her. There's something satisfying about how hard she freaks out when she thinks she's breaking a rule. I tell her I'm gonna look around a minute longer.

PETRA

Nolan was just being petulant by that point. I wasn't amused.

Neither was John. He was like, "I'm waiting outside. At least if something comes at me out there, I'll have a shot at getting away."

I followed him.

NOLAN

I look in a cupboard. Canned beans, canned peaches, bottled

water. Nothing interesting. I open the drawer in a battered night-stand, and it's got nothing in it but a jumbo bag of Tootsie Rolls. Then, when I'm shutting the drawer, I notice a Wilton newspaper on the bed—still rolled up and rubber-banded, but I can read the headline: *Popular Pizzeria Closes Following Kitchen Fire.*

I freeze.

I don't need to read the article to know the pizza place being referred to is Giuseppe's. It's been my favorite since I was a kid, so I've been bummed about it closing. That's not what has me shaken up, though. That's not what makes me decide that, yeah, I need to leave the cabin *immediately.*

Outside, I don't mention the newspaper. I'm not giving Petra the chance to get all self-righteous and smugly say she *told me so.* I casually let everyone know I'm done; we can go whenever they're ready.

But here's the thing: that pizzeria fire, it happened a week ago. A *week.* Someone's been in the cabin since then.

PETRA

By the time Nolan was done with his little trespassing endeavor, the sun was below the tree line. Exactly what I'd feared. I told everyone we needed to hustle.

[pause]

No, we didn't have trouble finding our way back to the campsite—that's mostly thanks to Abigail, if you must know. When we left the trail, I started to head in one direction, and she was like, "Actually, I think we're supposed to go this way."

She was right.

Going to the cabin, I'd been so focused on Nolan that I hadn't tracked our route. I let myself get disoriented, which, yes, was kind of embarrassing.

Whatever. I'm not perfect, okay?

Abigail ended up leading us all the way back to the creek. Who would have thought she'd be a freaking navigation expert?

ABIGAIL

Huh?

[pause]

I don't know how I got back to the campsite so easily. Good memory, I guess. Nana Abbie always says I have the memory of a dolphin—they remember things longer than any other animal. Well, except for humans.

But no one's going to use the phrase "memory of a human." That would just be weird.

15

The cabin seemed to give you some
misgivings. Did you consider going home?

PETRA

Why would we have gone home?

NOLAN

I'm a little unsettled after the cabin, yeah. But not because I
think we're in some sort of *danger*. I'm bothered because Petra
was right—we'd broken into someone's home. I'm kinda feeling
like a creep.

ABIGAIL

I didn't have any misgivings. I was just in a quiet mood, that's
all. I don't think anyone else was that bothered, either. Though
I don't know for sure, because I didn't go around asking every
single person—and who knows what anyone is *really* thinking?

My dad always says you can watch a buck from a blind and antic- ipate exactly what moves it's going to make, but humans are too tricky to guess about.

I think he was mostly talking about my mom when he said all that, though.

[pause]

But anyhow.

No. We didn't talk about going home.

JOHN

I suggested cutting the trip short. Obviously, that didn't happen.

PETRA

Did John tell you he tried to convince us to go home? That's why you're asking this, right?

[pause]

Just out of curiosity, are you going to answer *any* of my questions today? I mean, you must be sick of repeating "we can't share that information" by now.

God, don't you bore yourselves?

Anyway. Whatever.

While we were walking up the hill to the campsite, John was

like, "Think about it—if we leave now, we've got time to stop at that diner outside town, get some pancakes. Maybe catch a late movie. Go to sleep in our own beds without wondering what's watching us from the trees."

Maylee casually dropped, "Unless whoever's here follows us home. Even Jason ventures away from Camp Crystal Lake sometimes."

Nolan was slinking around the back of our group and muttered, "I can't believe we're having this conversation."

Obviously Maylee was like, "Says the guy who believes in *Bigfoot*."

At that point I stopped walking. I held up my hand to get everyone's attention and said, "Let's get a few things straight. There's a zero percent chance this forest is hiding either Bigfoot *or* a serial killer. I know you're worried, John, but that's not even how serial killers work. They don't hide in the woods hoping victims *come to them*."

Nolan said—and I swear, I could have killed him—he said, "Actually, there was a serial killer in Yosemite in the late nineties who operated just like that." He went on about how the killer was obsessed with Bigfoot and used that to lure his victims or something.

Everyone stared at Nolan like, um, do you think you're doing yourself any favors right now? Before I could tell him to keep that crap to himself, John started ticking off items on his fingers: "First we find a footprint. Then Nolan picks up a large animal on his thermal camera. Then we end up at a shack. Sorry, but this is adding up to a picture I don't want to be a part of."

Maylee sidled closer to him and said, "Don't forget all the noises we heard in the woods."

John nodded, like we'd undisputedly heard someone prowling the forest.

I was like, "Okay, my turn. There was no footprint. Nolan's thermal imager picked up a deer. The cabin is nothing. Did you see the turnoffs on the way here? There are probably a hundred similar cabins in these woods. You're seeing all the wrong kinds of danger lurking here. A serial killer, really? How about we discuss *bears*?"

John looked at me for a long moment, probably annoyed but too nice to show it. Finally, he said, "I'm just trying to prevent tomorrow's headline from being *Bodies of Five Wilton Teenagers Found Decapitated in Woods*."

I told him that *I* was just trying to prevent us from having to break down our campsite in the dark and drive all the way home a few hours after we'd arrived.

All reluctantly, as if she'd actually been contemplating leaving, Maylee said, "Petra's right. We should stay."

John raised his eyebrows and was like, "Really? You think it's safe?"

The rest of us stood around impatiently while Maylee gave him a speech about how she was sure the horror movie they'd watched was making their imaginations run wild, and logically speaking, there probably wasn't anything to be afraid of. *Probably.*

What finally convinced him was when she said, "I was really looking forward to spending the night with you. Who knows when we'll have this chance again?"

You should have seen how red Abigail's face got. I guess where she comes from, people don't even allude to having sex.

After a few more minutes of Maylee batting her eyelashes at him, John agreed to stay—though he clearly wasn't overjoyed about it. With that settled, we continued walking back to the campsite.

[pause]

Me? Honestly, I didn't give John's fears another thought. Nothing that had happened so far worried me.

Everything was great.

We were fine.

[pause]

God, I really hate being wrong.

16

Petra, you commented several times that
Maylee seemed unlike herself near the
cabin. Did you bring that up with her?

PETRA

How many hours have I been talking to you? Have you not
learned anything about me?

Obviously, I asked Maylee what was up.

She had her nose stuck in her phone, editing some photos
or something, but I managed to pry her away to collect firewood.
Once we were alone, I asked what her deal was. She said nothing.
I was like, "Maylee, you're my best friend. I know when you're
acting strange."

She was quiet for a second, then said, "What if John's right
and we're not alone out here? That cabin was creepy."

My first thought was, um, since when do you have a problem
with creepy things?

I mean, this is the girl who watches true crime documentaries to relax. In October, she makes me go to the haunted corn maze with her every weekend. Maylee says being scared makes her feel alive. Actually, she says *any* strong emotion makes her feel alive, even bad ones.

I remember a couple years ago, we were at this party, and, granted, she was a little...out of it. So maybe she wasn't making much sense. But she said to me, "Do you ever want to get into a fight with someone on purpose? Like, just because fighting would be fun?"

I was like, "Yeah, no. Fighting isn't entertaining to me."

Maylee thought about it and said, "It's not really about the fighting, actually. It's more about being angry. Sometimes it feels so good to be angry. Or sad. Like sometimes I want to feel so sad that it's like my heart is being sucked from my body."

I asked her why she would possibly want to feel that way.

She said, "I don't know. Just so I could feel *something*, I guess."

Anyway. I didn't mean to go on a tangent. I've been here for so long that I'm starting to talk like freaking Abigail Buckley. My point is, unlike John, I didn't buy that Maylee was scared of the cabin. When I told her as much, she was like, "You know what happens to girls like you in horror movies, Petra? They insist there's no danger right up to the moment it's too late."

I crossed my arms and gave her a look.

She bent down to gather some sticks. When she straightened up, she said, "Also, I've got a lot going on in my head right now. I'm getting a lot of content from this trip, and I'm trying to figure out how I want to use it."

[pause]

No, I didn't ask what she and Abigail had been whispering about. I told you, I was feeling sensitive about the whole thing. For all I knew they weren't really whispering and I was blowing things out of proportion.

[pause]

Yes, I eventually found out. But that was later.

[pause]

Actually, I *do* mind jumping ahead.

Look, I've been very forthcoming. I'm telling you crap that makes me uncomfortable or maybe paints me in a bad light. But I'm doing it anyway. Do you know why?

That was a rhetorical question. Obviously, I'm doing it because I'm willing to do anything if it'll help find Maylee.

But here's an idea: Considering that I'm fully cooperating with you, how about you back off and let me tell this the way I want to?

17

All right, let's get back to our timeline.
You've returned to the campsite. Then what?

ABIGAIL

It was getting cold by the time we got back to camp, so I put
my jacket on—I know it's really old and worn out, just like my
hiking boots, but it's so warm that I don't even care. After that, I
went over to watch Petra make the fire.

I hate to say this, because it doesn't sound very nice, but
gosh, she was way overcomplicating it. She was so super careful
about the kindling and how she piled the wood. It was like thirty
minutes before she even tried to light it.

I hope this doesn't sound like bragging, because Nana Abbie
says no one loves a show-off, but I could have done the same
thing as Petra in about three minutes. My dad says being able to
build a fire quickly is a skill everyone should have, like knowing
how to drive stick.

PETRA

It was one of my better campfires, actually. Abigail was hanging around while I made it, and I could tell she was impressed.

She asked me what we were having for dinner, and see, this is where I don't think people appreciate what I do enough. I planned all our food—and bought it, too, by the way. John was the only person who offered to chip in.

I figured we'd have hot dogs, because how much easier can you get? Until you factor in that Maylee needs some special hot dogs for her keto diet that can't be bought at the regular grocery store. And Nolan needs veggie dogs, but only a particular brand of veggie dogs. And John is fine with good old Ball Park Franks, but he needs gluten-free buns.

By the time I was done taking everyone's dietary restrictions into account, it was like I'd planned a freaking five-course meal.

ABIGAIL

We sat around the campfire and cooked our hot dogs. No one talked much, but it was in a relaxed way, not uncomfortable. At one point, Maylee leaned forward, so close to the flames that they nearly licked her face. She said, "Aren't campfires the best?"

John nudged her and said, "*You're* the best."

Maylee laughed and leaned into him.

They looked so in love right then.

It made me realize maybe I'd been hoping for more from Maylee than I'd let myself believe.

JOHN

Dinner was uneventful. Petra had gone out of her way to get everyone the right type of hot dog, which was very cool of her.

NOLAN

Petra makes sure to inform us that she went out of her way to find my favorite veggie dogs. The thing is, I'd told her beforehand that, sure, I have a preference, but as long as they're vegetarian, it doesn't really matter. She just has this thing where she wants so badly to be a martyr.

Besides that, dinner is chill. Even John stops glancing over his shoulder every two seconds. He starts telling us about the drama that goes on at student council meetings, and even though that's totally not my crowd, his stories are actually pretty hilarious.

But at one point, Maylee straight up interrupts him by leaning too close to the fire—she probably got tired of not being the center of attention. It works, because Abigail and Petra immediately tell her to back up, that she's gonna get burned. Maylee ignores them and says, "Fires are so great."

John gives her this sappy smile and says, "*You're* great."

Maylee's like, "Aw, you're sweet."

Then she asks him to take her picture.

PETRA

I watched John take Maylee's picture—which was like the fiftieth picture she'd asked him to take that day—and it struck me again how weird it was that Maylee wanted to camp somewhere without internet. Yeah, she could post the photos after the camping trip. But Maylee's never been one for delayed gratification.

JOHN

The fire was nice. While we were sitting there, for the first time, I felt like, okay, maybe I get why people like camping.

NOLAN

Since everything is casual and calm, I know I should keep my mouth shut. But I guess I'd been wanting to bring this up and wouldn't shake the urge until I did. So I'm like, "I really *did* see something on the thermal imager."

Everyone stops what they're doing. They're sitting there holding their food and staring at me and I'm having flashbacks to being eleven years old.

I say, because now that I've started, I can't stop, "Just in case anyone was wondering, something really was in the woods with us, giving off heat. Something big."

I wait for Petra to roll her eyes and say something sarcastic, try to tear me down. But instead she's calmly like, "There are a lot of deer around here, Nolan."

And that's worse, you know? Her treating me gently, that's about the worst thing she could do.

So I say, "I *know* there are a lot of deer. That's one of the reasons Salvation Creek has so much bigfoot activity. Large carnivores are naturally gonna live in areas with lots of prey."

Petra straight up cringes. John looks down at his hot dog like it's the most interesting thing he'd ever seen.

Then Abigail says, "Nolan, can I ask you something?"

She doesn't say it in a judgmental way. I can see she's just curious. Genuinely curious with no scorn. And it's like...I don't know. The longer we're in the woods, the happier I am to have Abigail around.

I tell her yeah, sure, she can ask anything.

ABIGAIL

I said, "Earlier, you mentioned a bunch of people who went missing or died here. And they had some...what did you call them?"

Nolan said, "Commonalities."

I was like, "Right, commonalities. But really, don't you think the thing the disappearances have *most* in common is just that they're all mysterious?"

PETRA

Abigail Buckley is smarter than she lets on.

ABIGAIL

I was only trying to point out that the disappearances were all so different from each other that I didn't see how Nolan could blame bigfoots for all of them. It didn't make sense.

Before Nolan could respond, Maylee laughed—and it was a mean laugh, one I didn't like much. She said, "Abigail, it doesn't make sense because there's no fucking bigfoot roaming the woods."

NOLAN

Ask me how many shits I give about Maylee's opinion.

No?

Well, the answer is zero.

Whether or not she believes in bigfoots has nothing to do with what I believe. So yeah, I don't care when she makes that snide comment. Abigail was talking to *me*. I say, "You're right, there's a lot that doesn't add up right now. I doubt we'll get all the answers until we find one of these creatures and study them."

Because that's how it goes, right? Most things don't make sense when you only have half the information.

PETRA

John put his hand on Maylee's knee, and I knew it was supposed to be a signal for her to chill out. I also knew there was no chance of that happening.

Maylee was like, "Nolan, I bet I can come up with an explanation for every disappearance you list. One that has nothing to do with Bigfoot."

I could tell the conversation was going to get heated in like two seconds. And while I normally don't shy away from confrontation—obviously—I had a feeling Nolan was going to end up hurt. So I said, "Anyone want another hot dog?"

John said, "I'll have one. Thanks. So where'd you end up buying these buns?"

Nolan ignored us and focused on Maylee. He said, "In several incidents, young children traveled huge distances. Like thirteen miles in an eight-hour period. How could they have gone so far on their own?"

Maylee rolled her eyes and said, "Have you spent any time around toddlers, Nolan? Those fuckers are fast."

JOHN

The conversation was becoming tense, yes. I tried changing the subject, but they weren't having it.

NOLAN

So then I bring up the missing people whose bodies are found in weird spots. I ask, what about the woman who was wedged tight into a tree trunk, stripped down to her underwear, her clothes folded neatly nearby?

Go ahead, explain *that*.

PETRA

Nolan looked pretty pleased with himself. He sat back in his camping chair and crossed his arms, waited for Maylee to come up with a theory. I could tell from her expression that the gears in her head were turning. But apparently she didn't get anywhere, because she said, "Petra, I bet *you* could explain it."

My heart sank.

She said, "Come on. You know everything about the woods."

In that moment, just for a second, I was furious. Maylee was putting me in the middle, purposely pitting me against my brother. It wasn't malicious or anything; she just wasn't thinking. She was amused by poking holes in Nolan's beliefs and couldn't step outside herself enough to see that he was actually bothered.

And I wanted—I *really* wanted—to stand behind Nolan.

If Maylee hadn't brought me into it, I would have silently sat through the conversation. But, like...I can't outright lie, okay? So I said, "There's nothing supernatural—or cryptozoological—about a body being wedged into a confined space."

Nolan snorted.

I said, "Really. It's caused by hypothermia. It's called hide-and-die syndrome."

John put down the hot dog he was eating. He said, "You all have some weird ideas about what makes appropriate dinner conversation."

Meanwhile, Nolan was already shaking his head, which killed my sympathy for him.

It would have taken him two seconds to research this himself. For *any* of his Bigfoot-hunter pals to research it. The fact that they hadn't was just negligent. And it's exactly why NACRO won't ever be taken seriously. They pick and choose which facts to hold up and disregard any information that doesn't fit their narrative.

Anyway, I kept talking, because by that point there was no turning back. I said, "We learned about it in the SAR class I took. When people reach the end stages of hypothermia—when they're close to dying—they get disoriented and often crawl into cramped spaces."

Nolan scowled and said, "I suppose they undress first, too?"

I was totally surprised when Abigail spoke up. She was like, "They do. My dad told me about it. I forget what it's called…"

I said, "Paradoxical undressing."

Abigail said, "Right! My dad says if I'm ever out in the snow and suddenly feel so warm that I want to take my clothes off to cool down, then I need to find shelter right away."

Nolan kept shaking his head. But that's the way it is with him. He already knows what he wants to believe, and no one will convince him otherwise.

JOHN

I didn't offer my opinion at the time.

But if you must know, when I hear about a naked woman's corpse shoved into a tree, I can't help but think it sounds pretty sinister.

PETRA

Nolan's desperate for some blanket theory that covers every person who ever went missing in the woods. And I get it. It's great when things are tied up in neat bows. But it's not that easy.

Life is messy.

It doesn't always have answers.

And the woods are freaking dangerous.

ABIGAIL

This one time, I was with my dad on a hunting trip. I don't know how old I was exactly, but I must have been pretty little because I know he hadn't let me shoot yet.

My dad was cleaning a deer, and I never liked that part. He says you have to do it right away, though, out in the field. Otherwise you risk ruining your meat. Since it was lunchtime, I decided I'd just go for a walk.

I wandered for a little bit, then sat down against a tree to eat my peanut butter and jelly sandwich and read the book I'd brought. It was fall, so the woods weren't super thick, not like in summer. There were some bushes near me, but I wasn't covered by them or anything.

After a little while, I heard my dad calling my name. For some reason, I ignored him. I really don't know why. I probably just wanted to keep reading longer. I'm kinda bad about ignoring everything around me when I'm in the middle of a book—especially when it's a romance and the main characters are just about to kiss for the first time.

Anyhow, my dad walked by—I saw him clearly even though he was wearing his camo jacket. Then he walked in the opposite direction. He crossed in front of me a bunch of times, practically circled the tree I was leaning against, shouting for me and looking around.

He couldn't see me.

I had on a blaze orange vest, the one he always makes me wear when we go into the woods. It was the middle of the day, and I wasn't trying to hide or anything.

But still, he walked right past.

When I could tell he was getting panicky, I jumped up and ran over to him. He hugged me so tight and he was shaking, and I realized just how scared he'd been.

It was a good lesson about how you can hurt people even if you don't mean to. And maybe an even better lesson about how easy it is to disappear in the forest. Even if you take precautions and someone knows right where you should be, when you're out in the trees and bushes and boulders, it's so, so easy to disappear.

PETRA

Nolan had the most stubborn look on his face. He was like, "I'm sorry, I just don't believe these disappearances are unrelated."

I guess I might have snapped a little. I was like, "Why are you being so willfully ignorant? Honestly, getting lost in the wilderness might be the easiest way to die. No one knows when they're entering a survival situation; don't you get that?"

There was a long silence.

No one was looking at each other, and John kept glancing

back at the woods like he expected some monster to come crawling out.

Maylee was the one who broke the tension. She stood up and said, "On that note, I'm ready for a drink. Anyone else?"

18

Clearly, Nolan is very committed to his belief in cryptids. Are you aware of any times this caused problems in his life?

PETRA

Um...did you even think about that question before asking it? We're talking about someone who believes in *Bigfoot*—and it's not like he tries to keep it a secret. Do I really need to tell you how high school is going for him?

ABIGAIL

I don't see Nolan around school very often, but I guess he probably gets made fun of. Which is really sad—and it's unfair, too, because no one can say for sure that bigfoots don't exist.

[pause]

Do *I* think they're real?

Honestly, before talking to Nolan, I kinda assumed that no one *truly* believed in them, like no one believes in unicorns. Or... *do* people believe in unicorns? Are there groups like the one Nolan's in, NARCO or whatever it is, only everyone is trying to find proof of unicorns? I guess they're so much like horses, it's not really *that* weird to think they might—

Huh?

[pause]

Oh, sorry.

Where was I?

[pause]

Right, okay. I never believed in bigfoots before, but a kinda weird thing is that during hunting trips, my dad always reminds me to be careful because the woods belong to animals and they can navigate way better than us. He says that some of the animals hiding in the brush would rip us apart just because we exist.

I figured he was talking about bears and cougars, but who knows? He's been hunting at Salvation Creek since he was little. Maybe he's seen something he couldn't explain.

So I guess that while I *mostly* don't think bigfoots are real, I'm not going to decide anything for sure.

Nana Abbie always says if you refuse to believe in something just because you can't see it, you'll live an empty life.

PETRA

Tell me this: If bigfoots or bigfeet or whatever the freaking plural is, if they exist, why haven't we found one? Because they're so hidden in the forest or something? Sure, fine. But then what about their bodies? They're living creatures, so they must die. And you're telling me that not once, in the entire history of this country, have we found a corpse?

Or...what? Am I supposed to believe they *bury* their dead?

JOHN

Nolan's beliefs are his own business.

[pause]

Out of curiosity, did he or Petra tell you about the Boy Scout camping trip the three of us went on when we were kids?

[pause]

I'm not getting deep into it, because it's not my story to tell. But what happened that night never sat right with me.

PETRA

Yes, I was a Boy Scout.

What, just because I have a vagina, I'm not allowed to learn survival skills?

19

Nolan, we'd like you to tell us about
the Boy Scout camping trip.

NOLAN
Why?

[pause]

Who even mentioned that to you? Petra?
I'm sure it was Petra.

[pause]

You know what's really uncool? Even after everything I've
told you guys, you're still sitting there judging me.

No, don't pretend you aren't. You smirk every time you say
the word *bigfoot*. It's all a big joke, isn't it? The blurry photos, the
stupid bumper stickers. Harry and the fucking Hendersons.

Why is the idea of an undiscovered species so unbelievable?

This continent is covered in forests, and huge sections of them are unexplored. How egotistical is it to assume we already know everything about places where no humans have set foot?

But sure, fine, go ahead and laugh at me. Everyone else is. You want to know about the Boy Scout trip, here's what happened:

I'm eleven years old. Ray makes me join Boy Scouts because Wilton is the kind of town where that's basically law. I try to get out of it by telling him my time would be better spent supporting an organization that's *not* run by homophobic bigots, but that doesn't go over well.

What's with that look? Are you an Eagle Scout or something?

Anyway, I end up joining the troop, and it's not *completely* unbearable. I get my Reading and Astronomy badges. We do some okay crafts, some interesting science experiments. But the outdoorsy shit is pure torture—and there's no way to avoid the annual camping trip. I don't want anything to do with it. I hate the idea of sleeping in a tent and hiking through the woods. I don't want to be in the sun all day—or even worse, in the rain. I can't imagine an activity more mind-numbing than fishing.

Those weren't the only issues. My Boy Scout troop was filled with these super athletes—you know, the type of kid *you* probably were. And there I am, this skinny nerd who'd rather be reading a book than playing sports.

You can probably guess how well I fit in. The other guys

aren't too obvious about it, not with my stepdad being the troop leader, but yeah, they make fun of me. Of course they make fun of me.

I beg Ray to let me skip the camping trip—but I'm eleven; my negotiation skills aren't exactly top notch. Ray tells me it would be silly to do Scouts all year then back out of this big event. My mom agrees with whatever Ray says, and when I try to talk to my dad about it, he says, "Don't rock the boat."

My dad's a decent guy, but when it comes to anything related to the divorce and our blended families, his response is to not rock the boat. It makes me wonder, does he think our situation is so precarious that it could all fall apart because of something as small as not wanting to go on a camping trip?

Fine, though. I listen. I don't rock the boat.

So I end up on this camping trip with a bunch of people I don't like. I can't relate to any of them about anything. And Petra's not making it any easier.

The second she starts tagging along—because God forbid she do anything as traditional as join *Girl* Scouts—she appoints herself the de facto leader. At first the guys are amused at having a girl around, plus they respect her because she's better at basically everything than everyone. But they get sick of being ordered around real fast.

That's how it always is with Petra. People respect her; they just don't like her. I think Maylee might have been her only real friend.

Anyway, the camping trip starts off fine—well, it sucks, but I'm dealing with it. I'm mostly able to keep to myself, hiding behind a tree reading a book or working on a map. At that age, I was real into drawing maps. Maps of anything. Like, I'd draw maps of my houses. I was weird, okay?

Everything is fine until nighttime. I wake up at two a.m. or something with my bladder about to burst. And I'm terrified of going into the woods alone. We're supposed to use the buddy system if we leave the tent to go to the bathroom, but like I said, the other guys aren't my friends. If I wake one of them up because I'm too scared to do my business on my own, they'll kill me.

I decide to hold it until morning, but ten minutes later I know that's just not gonna be possible. The thought of wetting my sleeping bag is even worse than my fear of the woods. So I pull jeans and a sweatshirt over my pajamas and leave the tent.

The campfire is long dead. It's cold as shit and I can't see a thing. My flashlight is basically useless. I step away from the campsite, but just barely. I don't want to piss in the middle of camp, but I'm sure as hell not walking deep into the trees.

I unzip my jeans, shivering, at the same time aiming my flashlight around to make sure nothing is creeping out of the woods.

A branch breaks. I'm not talking about a little twig snapping. A *branch*. I startle so bad that my urine stream goes wild and I soak my foot. Then there's another sound. It's somewhere between a hoot and a howl. A strange *oooowhoo* sound. Nothing like any animal I've heard before.

I realize that aside from the snapping branch, aside from the weird animal call, the forest is silent. There'd been bugs chirping before. Birds or squirrels or something rustling leaves. You don't realize how noisy the world is until suddenly it's not. The silence is unnatural. My hands start to shake.

I want to get out of there. I rush to finish peeing, drop my flashlight like a klutz, try to pick it up at the same time that I'm zipping my pants. I'm getting frantic because I feel like I'm being watched. I'm almost certain I'm being watched.

Suddenly, in all that silence, a new sound.

An exhale of breath.

I freeze.

Something is in the darkness ahead of me. Right ahead of me. It can't be ten feet away.

I start to back up.

I don't shine my light at the thing, because I don't want to see it. I don't want to know what's standing there. A bear, maybe. Some other animal with sharp teeth and claws, ready to rip me apart. Or maybe even worse: a human. Even in my fear,

I'm praying it's not a human. An animal might just be curious about me, but a *person* lurking in the shadows, watching but not speaking...

I'm still walking backward, and I trip. Of course I do. I'm always tripping over my own feet. I land hard on my ass, the flashlight beam swings up—at the same moment, the thing in the trees moves forward and the light reflects off its eyes. Reflects a blue glow back at me. The creature takes another step, and that's when I see its face.

It's not a bear. Or a human. Or like anything I've ever seen before. It's tall; maybe seven, eight feet. Covered with matted, mangy fur that's got leaves and twigs stuck in it. It smells like sewage. Like rotting meat. Its face is leathery and wrinkled. It has long yellow teeth. I think it might have a snout.

It's like an ape and a human and a wolf all together.

It's the most horrible thing I've ever seen.

The way it's looking at me, it's not just hungry. It's like the creature hates me. *Hates* me. And I know it wants to kill me.

You ever heard of a guy named Grover Krantz? He was an anthropologist and professor. Also one of the most respected bigfoot researchers of all time. He was always trying to get a bigfoot corpse to study, and once someone asked him, "What's the first thing you'd do if you shot a bigfoot?"

And you know what he said?

"Reload."

In the woods that night, the bigfoot starts reaching for me. I don't even entertain the possibility that I can fight it off. So I close my eyes and start screaming. I scream and scream and scream.

I don't know how much time passes before I feel hands on me. Human hands. I open my eyes, and it's Ray. He's shaking me, saying my name over and over. I try to catch my breath. I look around. The entire Boy Scout troop, everyone in their pajamas and shivering, is staring at me.

Ray says, "What happened, Nolan?"

I don't consider lying. Why the fuck would I lie? I tell everyone what I saw and say we need to get out of the woods before the creature comes back. Before it slaughters every last one of us.

I'm sitting there in the cold, cowering in the dirt, my foot covered in my own piss. Everyone stares. And then someone laughs. Ray hushes them. Kids start whispering.

Yeah, you're not some innocent eleven-year-old, so you can probably guess where this is going. Ray's a good guy. He maintains that I saw some sort of animal out there. He says maybe it was even a bear. He tells the story in a way to make it sound like I was probably in danger, like I had every right to freak out as bad as I did.

Other people aren't so cool.

The rest of the troop—even Petra—they think I overre-acted to some bad nightmare. That maybe I was sleepwalking or something.

And yeah, I get made fun of for it. For a year at least. Even now, every once in a while, some asshole will randomly be like, "Hey Nolan, remember the time you saw a monster in the woods?"

For a long time I'm convinced that maybe Ray is right. Maybe it was a normal animal and my sleepy, scared brain turned it into some atrocity.

Then, a few years later, I learn about bigfoots. Well, I *knew* about them already—you grow up in the Pacific Northwest and you're very familiar with the legends. But I always thought about them the way you probably do. Like a big joke. Then I see a documentary about Grover Krantz and I realize there are people—*scientists*—who take bigfoots seriously. And during the documentary, people talk about their own encounters, and I realize it's the same thing I experienced. It's *exactly* what I experienced.

You know what gets me the most? The eyeshine. That refers to the way animals' eyes glow when they reflect light. Different animals have different color eyeshine. For instance, bears have yellow, and wolves have white.

There's no known biped that has blue eyeshine. Except for bigfoots.

I start doing my own research, and that's how I find NACRO. That's how I actually connect with people who have encountered bigfoots. That's how I find out about the clusters of strange disappearances and the commonalities and...all of it.

The best part is, the more I dive into research, the more all the issues I had after the camping trip—the nightmares and stuff—start to go away. My head feels less screwed up all the time. And I guess that's when I start to think that instead of just reading about bigfoots, wouldn't it be great if I actually *found* one?

20

All right, let's get back to—

PETRA

Hold up.

I want to say one more thing about Bigfoot, okay?

I think you should know that when we were kids, when Nolan had his weird experience in the woods, he called the thing he saw a werewolf.

It wasn't until way later, after he saw some Bigfoot documentary, that he suddenly remembered the creature looking different.

I don't mean that he's lying.

He believes that he saw Bigfoot. Really.

I'm just saying that maybe the thing he remembers seeing today isn't the same thing he *always* remembered seeing.

Memory is funny like that.

21

Maylee brought alcohol on the camping
trip, correct? We need to know who
was drinking and how much.

PETRA

I don't drink alcohol.

[pause]

God, *yes*, that's the truth.

I look forward to having a drink when I turn twenty-one, but in the meantime, I'm not interested in breaking the law.

ABIGAIL

I don't really drink. I have before, but just a couple of times. My dad always says he doesn't want to ever catch me with alcohol in my system because it's a slippery slope and addiction runs in our family.

So, anyhow, I wasn't drinking on the camping trip.

Except for maybe a few sips.

But that doesn't count, right?

[pause]

Are you sure I won't get in trouble for this?

JOHN

My lawyer advises me not to answer that question.

NOLAN

I had a few beers. And whatever Maylee kept pouring into my sodas. Whiskey, I think.

PETRA

Nolan's such a lightweight that he doesn't even know the difference between whiskey and rum.

I suppose it makes sense. When would he have even encountered alcohol before? It's not like he goes to parties. His NACRO buddies aren't exactly sharing drinks through the internet.

NOLAN

No, it wasn't my first time having alcohol.

[pause]

It was my second.

And okay, sure, the first time was when my dad let me have a beer last year during the Superbowl. I had to choke it down, if you want to know the truth.

Last night, at Salvation Creek, it was a lot better. I was prepared for the taste.

[pause]

I bet Petra told you that I'm not used to alcohol because I don't have friends to drink with, didn't she? For the record, I *do* have friends at school. Not a lot. But I have them.

Ask her how many friends *she* has. Seriously, actually ask her. She sits with the popular crowd at lunch and goes to parties and stuff. But that's only because of Maylee. Who else does she actually have a relationship with?

JOHN

Yes, I can confirm that Maylee was drinking—more than I was comfortable with. I suggested that she take it easy. Abigail did, too. At one point I overheard her tell Maylee something like, "Don't get drunk; it'll mess everything up."

[pause]

I had no idea what she was talking about.

It's possible I misheard her.

PETRA

We were sitting around the fire—except for Maylee, who'd gone to the cooler—when Abigail was like, "Is everyone done eating? If so, we should maybe move the food away from the campsite so it doesn't attract bears."

Which, yes, *obviously* I was going to suggest. I just hadn't gotten to it yet.

John said he'd help her, and the two of them packed up everything except for the marshmallows. I was pleasantly surprised to see them talking and laughing while they did it. Kind of a big change, considering a few hours before, Abigail acted nervous every time he spoke to her.

I grabbed a stick and was using it to turn the logs for more oxygen flow when Maylee wandered back to the campfire. She went up to Nolan and was like, "Looks like someone's ready for a top-off," and poured more rum into his cup.

When she came over to me, she wasn't stumbling, exactly, but walking a little too loosely. I lowered my voice and said, "Watch it with Nolan, okay? He's not used to alcohol."

Maylee said, "Um, yeah, that's kind of the point? Trust me, this is going to be hilarious."

I found nothing funny about the situation. I've been to

parties where people act like it's a game to get other kids wasted and record them or whatever, but to me that's just really irresponsible. I told Maylee, "Seriously, cut it out. It's dangerous to get drunk out here. You should slow down, too, by the way."

She rolled her eyes and said, "Killjoy."

She didn't mean it though, you know? That's just our thing. She always goes too far—with everything—and I reel her back. And I act like I'm exasperated by her antics, and she acts like I'm ruining her fun, but that's just part of the dynamic. Like a skit we've performed so many times that we know the lines by heart.

Maylee sat down next to me, plopped in the dirt too hard. And then she said—

[pause]

Actually, I can't remember what she said.

NOLAN

Maylee said the weirdest fucking thing to Petra by the fire. Did Petra tell you?

She pulls out her phone and says, "I have so many good pictures on here."

Petra's like, "Yes, Maylee, you're very photogenic," or some garbage like that.

And Maylee says, "Will you promise me something? If you ever need a picture of me and I'm not around to give you one, go into my phone and choose the picture taken last August at the lake. It's a head-and-shoulders shot with the water behind me. I'm wearing a blue shirt and my hair is down."

And I'm thinking, *what* is she talking about?

And Petra says, "What are you talking about?"

Maylee is all, "Just if you ever need one, okay?"

Petra asks why that would possibly happen.

Maylee looks her straight in the eyes and says, "What if I die or something and my mom needs a picture for the obituary? She'd pick something totally wrong, like my school photo. That doesn't even look like me."

I glance at my sister, and she seems about as baffled as I am. She's like, "Since when does alcohol make you so morbid?"

Maylee says, "Just promise, okay? Choose the lake picture—or another one that John took, if you have to. He takes the best pictures of me."

I'm guessing Maylee is drunker than I realized. Petra must have the same thought. She nods once, goes back to poking at the fire, and says, "Yes, Maylee. I promise."

PETRA

I tore open the package of marshmallows, took a couple, then offered the bag to Maylee. She was like, "I'm not eating straight sugar, Petra."

As if she weren't constantly snacking on candy. Whatever. I'm not making her diet my business unless I think she's hurting herself.

John was just getting back to the campfire, and he snatched the bag from me and said, "I, meanwhile, am more than happy to eat Maylee's share."

Then—and this is the part I still can't believe—*Nolan* took the bag and, I swear, slid like four marshmallows onto a skewer. I said, "You know these aren't vegetarian, right? They've got gelatin in them."

But he went ahead and ate them anyway.

That's when I realized my brother was *very* drunk.

NOLAN

While everyone else was roasting marshmallows, Maylee came over and was like, "Uh-oh, you're empty again."

I looked down at my cup and she was right, which kinda confused me because I didn't remember drinking that much. Maybe I spilled it or something. Anyway, she gave me some more whiskey.

[pause]

What? No, I didn't eat any marshmallows. They smelled good, though. I wish Petra would have looked for a vegetarian option.

ABIGAIL

After John and I stashed the food, I told him I'd meet him back at the campsite and went into the woods to pee. I don't like having to squat—half the time I swear I end up peeing on myself a little—but I've spent enough time in the forest that I'm used to it.

As I was pulling my pants back up, I happened to look at the sky. It was a full moon. I've always loved full moons. The night was chilly and the air was damp, and it smelled like pine and burned marshmallows—gosh, is there anything more warm and cozy than marshmallows over the fire?

I did my last button and was about to go back to the group when I heard a noise in the forest. A branch cracking, maybe. I turned quickly and peered into the shadows. For a second I got this really uncomfortable feeling that someone was out there and had just seen me pee. Which would be kinda embarrassing and creepy at the same time.

But I stood still and listened closely, and there weren't any more noises. Then I felt really silly for letting myself get scared. I finished adjusting my clothes and headed back to the group.

At the edge of the campsite, I paused for a second. The

flickering fire made everyone's shadows stretch long, all the way to where I stood. I heard the hum of their voices but couldn't make out what they were saying. There was a lot of talking, though—happy-sounding talking. Every once in a while, someone laughed.

The scene was so...peaceful, I guess. I couldn't see any of the tension or weirdness or fears or lies that had happened earlier that day. Instead, it was like watching this easy friend-magic. Everyone gathered late at night, sipping drinks, eating junk food, just being together far away from the rest of the world.

And I was a part of it. I'd been invited on the camping trip. I belonged with the group. Even knowing how everything else turned out, when I think back about that moment, it still feels good.

22

Did anything notable happen while
you were toasting marshmallows?

PETRA

Not really. Abigail and Nolan debated the proper amount of char on the outside of a marshmallow. John pretended to sip the same beer that was just as full as when he'd opened it an hour before.

For a while, everything was really good. We hung out, talked, ate. It was exactly how I'd imagined the camping trip. Everyone just relaxing and enjoying nature and each other's company.

Then Maylee said we should play Truth or Dare.

I freaking hate Truth or Dare.

JOHN

No one wanted to play Truth or Dare. Maylee suggested Spin the Bottle instead.

I consider myself a laid-back guy, right? I didn't have an

issue with Maylee and Abigail's friendship. I was even okay with Abigail being on the camping trip. But I have limits. I told Maylee, "I'm sorry, but I'm not comfortable playing Spin the Bottle with your ex."

PETRA

Maylee was going through all these games. Truth or Dare, Never Have I Ever, Two Truths and a Lie. And the rest of us were saying no, no, no.

Then she mentioned Spin the Bottle and John said, "No way am I playing Spin the Bottle with your ex."

Maylee laughed, and for a second I laughed, too. Because it must have been a joke, right? John was saying that Maylee had... what? Dated Nolan?

If it was a joke, it wasn't really funny.

Maybe John was drinking more than I realized.

ABIGAIL

I stopped moving. I almost couldn't breathe.

She'd told John.

How could she have told John?

NOLAN

Sure, I knew about Maylee and Abigail. Last year or...the year before? I can't remember. But a while back, I had to go to the nurse's office during PE. I had a migraine that prevented me from participating in class. Darn.

On my way there, I passed the two of them. They were in this stairwell nook and didn't notice me because they were making out. I didn't think that much of it because who cares who's hooking up with who? I told you I'm not into that high school drama bullshit.

Why?

Was it supposed to be a secret?

ABIGAIL

Maylee was the one who wanted to keep our relationship secret, not me. I would have told everyone in the world. But I kept quiet, like she wanted.

I *mostly* kept quiet, anyhow. I did tell my dad. But that's my dad, you know? I don't think he counts. Besides, it's not like I could've hid it from him. The day after Maylee and I kissed for the first time, he and I went fishing and while we were out there, I couldn't stop smiling.

He kept saying, "You gonna fill me in on whatever it is so I can smile, too?"

It was a warm spring day—one of those days that feels more like summer. The creek sparkled, and there was something sweet, like flowers, mixing with the smell of my dad's tobacco. I felt all drowsy and dazed and happy.

Anyhow, I ended up telling him about Maylee. He was happy for me. He's always happy about things that make me happy.

[pause]

Huh?

No, my dad's not like that.

Gosh, everyone always thinks the most awful things about him. I guess some of his views are kinda unusual. But as he always says, just because he believes in personal freedom and limited government doesn't mean he's a bigot.

You know, a bunch of people at school have asked how he reacted when I came out to him—as if it's any of their business. And the weird thing is, the way they say it, I know they're only asking because they think he threatened to disown me or something, and they want to hear all the gory details.

It didn't happen like that. The truth is, one day my dad was sorting through paperwork, grumbling again about what a mess my mom made because she ran off but never actually divorced him. He said something like, "Find yourself a partner, Ab, but steer clear of marriage. It ain't nothing but a hassle." I said to him, "I don't think I'd like a husband anyhow." He glanced at me for a second and was like, "I said *marriage*, not husband." And that was that.

So when I told my dad about me and Maylee, he wasn't surprised I was dating a girl or anything. But he did say, "If anyone at Sunny Acres gives you trouble—even if they just make a comment that don't sit right, you tell me."

I told him that no one at Sunny Acres would even know, because Maylee and I weren't going public just yet. He asked why not. And I said the same thing Maylee had told me. It wouldn't be as special if everyone knew.

My dad looked at me for a long time. Finally, he said, "You be careful with this girl, Ab."

And I was—

[pause]

Wait. Why did I even bring this up?

Oh! Right.

I was just saying that no one knew about Maylee and me dating.

Almost no one.

PETRA

Maylee was a big fan of secret relationships. She wanted some Romeo and Juliet thing, only there was no reason for that in her life, so sometimes she tried to invent problems. I called her on it once, on trying to make her relationships unnecessarily dramatic. Her response was something like, "It's just that once you get past the part where you admit to liking each other, it gets really boring."

So yes, she'd had secret relationships before, but she wasn't keeping them secret from *me*.

And she *never* would have dated Nolan.

[pause]

What?

[pause]

John meant...

[pause]

Maylee and *Abigail*?
Oh my God, that makes so much more sense.

ABIGAIL

I guess after a while the sneaking around started to bug me. I wondered if there was another reason Maylee didn't want people to know about us—but what? She'd dated other girls before, so people at school knew she was bi. And I'm sure she wasn't dating someone else at the same time—that's what my dad was worried about, that I was, like, a side girlfriend.

Eventually, I got so sad about hiding our relationship that I gave Maylee an ultimatum. I don't think ultimatums are probably ever good, you know? Like, by the time I needed to give her one, things were already too messed up to fix.

I told Maylee that we either had to be together publicly or break up.

She cried a lot. A whole lot. More than I did, even. She told me all these things about how she'd always care about me and how much I meant to her.

I think about three weeks after that is when she started dating John.

PETRA

I just...I'm sorry. I still don't understand why she wouldn't have told me.

23

It seems like you might not have known
Maylee as well as you thought, Petra.
Maybe on the camping trip, that was starting to upset you? Maybe it started to
upset you even *before* the trip?

PETRA

Oh my God.

I did not hurt Maylee.

I *did not* hurt her.

She's my best friend and I love her.

Yes, maybe there are some things I didn't know about her.
But no one ever knows someone else completely. Everyone puts
on fronts or tries to present themselves the way they want to be
seen. Don't act like you don't do it, too.

We all tell stories about the people we want to be.

24

Did you end up playing Spin the Bottle?

JOHN

No. Maylee gave up on that idea fairly fast.

PETRA

We didn't end up doing anything. The mood changed. I was still wondering what John meant with that ex comment. Nolan was getting drunker. Abigail was lost in her own world.

And Maylee was getting bored.

ABIGAIL

I couldn't stop thinking about it—that Maylee had told John about her and me. After all that secrecy, why tell him?

It made me feel trivial.

It made me feel like a footnote in her life.

It made me wonder why I was on the camping trip at all.

NOLAN

I remember the marshmallows. I remember Maylee pouring the rest of the whiskey into my cup. After that everything is kinda a blur.

PETRA

It's never a good thing when Maylee gets bored. She reminds me of the border collie my family had when I was little. Freya was a good dog, but she was too smart and had too much energy. If we didn't keep her entertained, she'd get bored, and when she got bored, she destroyed things.

JOHN

I left the campfire and went to my tent. I wasn't planning on being gone long—ten minutes, maybe. Just enough to get a break from being social. It can be tiring sometimes.

The last thing on my mind was snooping through Maylee's things. I've never gone through her phone or read her emails. But she'd left a notebook open on her sleeping bag, and yeah, I admit I glanced at it.

At first, I thought it was a post she was drafting about the camping trip. Except it was about things that hadn't happened, like getting lost in the woods. I didn't read the entire thing, though. I felt guilty for looking at all.

[pause]

No, as far as I know, Maylee had never written fiction before.

[pause]

Yes, I *do* find it weird, considering. And I—

[pause]

My lawyer advises me not to answer questions based on speculation.

PETRA

Maylee mixed another rum and Coke and said, "Truth or Dare, Abigail?"

Abigail shook her head and was like, "Huh-uh. Last time we played Truth or Dare, you dared me to post a selfie, and I got all those creepy messages from guys I don't even know."

Um, pardon me?

When exactly had *that* happened?

Before I could ask, Maylee said, "It was like three DMs. That's nothing. But pick truth if it makes you more comfortable."

On the other side of the fire, Nolan was slumped down so far in a camp chair that I thought he'd fallen asleep. He startled me when he snorted and said, "Nothing about this trip has been *comfortable*."

Maylee ignored him. She took a swig of her drink, then

looked at Abigail and said, "I'll give you an easy question: Do you like John better now that you've spent some time with him?"

Abigail's face went red and her shoulders hunched in even more than usual. She mumbled something about how she didn't *dislike* John before.

Maylee said, "You don't need to lie. It's okay to dislike people."

Nolan was like, "Wow, thanks for giving us permission."

At least, I think that's what he said. It was hard to tell through the slurring.

I wasn't really overjoyed with the turn the conversation was taking, so I clapped my hands and said, "Let's do something. I brought a deck of cards."

Maylee was like, "Fucking *cards*, Petra? I'm talking about something important, and you want to play Go Fish?"

I said, "You're not talking about anything important. You're drunk."

She *was* drunk, okay?

I'm not excusing her actions or anything, just trying to explain the situation. If Maylee was sober, she might have amused herself by stirring up trouble, but she *never* would've said what she did next. Which was "Do you know that Abigail thinks John was driving the night Andy Snyder almost died?"

It was seriously messed up to bring up the accident like that. Seriously. I glanced toward the tent to make sure John hadn't come back—but, I mean, it's not like he was behind soundproof walls.

I said, "Let it go, Maylee."

She turned to Abigail and was like, "You think it's all John's fault, right? That's what your dad told you. He's friends with Andy's mom—did you know that, Petra? Abigail's dad was at the hospital when people were making that big scene."

Abigail swallowed hard. She spoke so quietly that I had to strain to hear her say, "You don't know anything about my dad."

Maylee snapped, "I know he's a right-wing extremist, and I know he thinks John is a criminal. Seems like that's enough."

There was a long, awful silence.

I glanced at Abigail, expecting her to, I don't know, pull even further into herself or something. But she had this fierce look on her face. She said, "My dad's a libertarian, and if you think that's the same as being a right-wing extremist, you should do some research. And none of that has anything to do with John's accident."

I was so surprised she stood up to Maylee, I almost fell over.

But good for her, right?

Even if I think she's probably wrong, good for her.

ABIGAIL

I guess you know about the accident already?

Maybe it was John's fault; maybe not. But that didn't have anything to do with what I saw on the camping trip.

John went into the woods and came back with Maylee's blood on his hands. No matter what happened before, last night he was a killer.

PETRA

Nolan perked up then, which, God, was *just* what we needed. He leaned forward—practically fell out of his freaking chair before catching himself—and said, "Jesus, Maylee, why are you such a bitch?"

Have you ever seen a nature documentary where it shows the exact moment a predator locks on to its prey? When Maylee looked at Nolan, it was like that. She laughed and said, "I don't know, why are *you* so pathetic?"

And then she just went off. Taunting him about his Bigfoot crap, saying NACRO is a huge group of losers. She said, "What are you even going to do if you find Bigfoot, huh? You're so useless, you'd probably lie down and wait for it to kill you."

Nolan tried to respond, but it was basically just a garbled string of expletives.

Maylee was like, "Let's face it, Nolan. You're just another basement-dwelling incel creep who lives in a fantasy because your reality is too pitiful to face."

NOLAN

I...

I guess that happened?

I remember some of it, like Maylee calling me useless. But the rest...

[pause]

If everyone else says it happened, I'm sure it did.

ABIGAIL

I don't think I've ever seen anyone be as cruel as Maylee was last night. It was sad and scary, and, gosh, I was *furious* at her.

[pause]

It feels weird to admit that now, after everything that's happened. Because even though Maylee was being awful, I don't know, it seems unfair to say so when she never got a chance to explain herself or apologize.

And she *would* have. I'm sure of it. Last night she was nervous and drunk and didn't know what she was doing.

Honestly, I was feeling a little cloudy, too.

PETRA

At that point, I considered dragging John out of his tent. I didn't want to deal with being the only sober person at the campfire.

ABIGAIL

There's also a part of me that wonders...

Okay, this might sound silly. But sometimes Maylee used to talk about things like fate and premonitions. She swore that her dreams sometimes came true. She posted this thing once where she talked about how everyone is born knowing their own future, it's just that most of us don't know how to put the pieces together.

What if...don't laugh, but what if Maylee knew she was going to die? What if part of her *really* knew it? And when she started saying that terrible stuff, she was trying to make us hate her just so losing her would be easier?

PETRA

Once, years ago, Maylee said, "Do you ever hate me?"

I said no, of course not.

She asked if I ever thought I should.

We were walking home from the movie theater. It was a dusky evening in spring and the air smelled like honeysuckle and fresh laundry. The last thing on my mind was hating my best friend. I said, "Do you *want* me to hate you?"

She said, "I don't know. Sometimes I think it would be good to be hated. Hated or loved. Nothing in between."

I thought of that conversation last night when she was poking at people's weaknesses, trying to rile everyone up. I'd seen her do similar stuff before—at school or parties or wherever. When I called her on it, she'd say, "I'm making people's lives more interesting, Petra—I'm doing a *service*. Everyone wants drama. That's why we watch TV and read books."

But even though her little game was nothing new, last night she took it to a different level. The things she said to Nolan were vicious. I guess that's why it bothered me in a way it never had before. And why, at that moment, for the first time, I saw how someone could hate her.

ABIGAIL

Maylee kept going on and on about Nolan not having friends. And he—it was actually really weird—he leaped up from the camp chair and kinda lurched forward, but instead of moving toward Maylee, he moved toward *Petra* and shouted, "I'm so sick of you calling me a loser."

NOLAN

What? No. I didn't yell at Petra.

PETRA

He came at me like he'd been storing all of this up for like the last decade, yelling that he's sick of me treating him like he's a loser. And I was just like, "*Maylee* was the one talking, not me."

ABIGAIL

Nolan went on and on, shouting that Petra has always thought she was superior to him and that he's tired of her bossing him around. He said that she's abrasive and controlling, and the only reason anyone puts up with her is because of Maylee.

He said that she's so pathetic and friendless that there wasn't a single person she could invite on the camping trip besides her brother.

He said she clings to Maylee because Maylee is the only thing she has in the world.

PETRA

I didn't respond to Nolan.

[pause]

I guess because maybe he was right.

ABIGAIL

The whole time, Petra was so calm. She didn't yell back, not even once. Nolan was right up in her face and she just stood there, and I could tell that every word he said felt like getting hit.

NOLAN

No, I'm sure I wouldn't have said any of that to Petra.

I might have *thought* it when I was really mad.

But I never would've said it.

ABIGAIL

Maylee stood there watching the whole thing. She was…

Okay, it was hard to tell with the firelight and the smoke and the darkness. But I swear she was smiling.

When she finally stepped forward, I thought, oh good, she'll put a stop to this. But instead, she waited for Nolan to pause to take a breath and said, "Petra, can I borrow your ChapStick?"

Petra just nodded toward her tent and said, "It's in my backpack."

Maylee wandered away to find it, like she didn't have a care in the world.

PETRA

Was I upset?

God.

If you want to turn this into some heart-to-heart where I weep out my feelings to you, I'm going to need more coffee.

Let me just...

[pause]

Okay, imagine this:

Imagine there's a mirror, and when you look into it, it reflects back all the worst parts of yourself. The parts you convinced yourself can't possibly be as bad as you imagine. The parts you thought were hidden so deep that only you knew about them. Only when you look in this mirror, you find out those things had been totally visible the entire time.

[pause]

So yes.

I was upset.

JOHN

I was lying in the tent when I heard shouting. It sounded like Nolan. I got up to see what was going on.

ABIGAIL

I kept asking Nolan to calm down, but he wasn't listening, and then John showed up and yelled, "What the hell is going on out here?"

I guess he was trying to help, but it made the situation feel even more tense.

PETRA

Abigail and John were trying to get Nolan's attention, but he was so wrapped up in the hate he was spewing that he didn't notice. I thought about slapping him, snapping him right out of the moment.

I didn't, though.

I didn't do anything.

Stopping him seemed pointless. He'd already inflicted the damage he meant to.

It didn't matter in the end. He got the equivalent of a slap to the face a second later when the gun was fired.

25

Why did you bring the gun, Petra?

PETRA

Okay, I get that this looks bad. I know what you must be thinking.

But I'm telling you, it was totally innocent. I was going into a forest with people who had zero wilderness-survival skills. There are a lot of wild animals around Salvation Creek. And Nolan is right, there have been strange disappearances in the area. I brought the gun as a precaution.

And for the record, I wasn't running through the woods waving a Glock around with no idea how to use it. My dad's been taking me shooting since I was old enough to hold a gun. He used to take me and Nolan to the range every weekend, and it wasn't just target practice; he taught us gun safety, too. We both know how to handle ourselves with a firearm.

I just hadn't accounted for Maylee digging through my bag and finding it.

Let alone *firing* it.

There are three freaking safeties, I didn't even think she'd know how to bypass them.

[pause]

Oh my God, *obviously* my dad didn't give me permission to take the gun. What kind of question is that?

26

What happened after Maylee fired the gun?

JOHN

I didn't realize it was a gunshot. Not at first.

ABIGAIL

There was no mistaking the sound of the gunshot. The second I heard it, my whole body tensed up.

I've never fired a handgun. My dad hates them. He says everyone has the right to own a gun, but in his opinion rifles are used for hunting animals and handguns are used for hunting people.

But there's an alley behind Sunny Acres where people fire at cans, so I knew what a shot sounded like.

JOHN

I looked around the clearing and saw Maylee with a gun in her hand. You could say I was very uncomfortable with the situation.

PETRA

Maylee was standing near my tent, pointing the pistol at the sky, trying to look like Billy the freaking Kid or something—though being so obviously unprepared for the recoil kinda ruined the effect.

When she saw us looking, Maylee grinned and said, "Thought that would get your attention."

NOLAN

I kinda remember this part, though it's hazy.

Maylee's holding a gun, and it's like my brain can't quite process what I'm seeing. Especially because I know that gun. I've *fired* that gun.

I say, "Holy shit, Petra, what were you thinking?"

PETRA

It's my dad's off-duty gun, for the record. I didn't borrow his service weapon, for God's sake.

JOHN

I was thinking, "This is bad. This is *so* bad."

ABIGAIL

Every time we go hunting, before we even get started, my dad reminds me of how important firearm safety is. If you're not careful and don't treat your weapon with respect, everything could go very wrong very fast.

And the thing about Maylee is, even though I thought she was usually really great and even though I cared about her so much, I didn't trust her with a loaded gun.

PETRA

I told Maylee to put the gun down. She said, "I kinda like it, though."

She passed it from hand to hand, like she was admiring the heft of it.

I said, "This isn't a joke. *Put it down.*"

She gave me the biggest grin and said, "Here, catch."

My blood ran cold.

As she moved to toss the gun to me, I instinctively lunged forward. I stumbled, getting too close to the fire, nearly singeing my sleeve. I jerked my arm back from the flames just as Maylee said, "Careful there."

She still had the gun in her hand.

She'd never really meant to throw it.

It was all a game to her.

ABIGAIL

I think the only one of us who wasn't furious at Maylee was

Nolan and only because he was too drunk to really know what was going on.

JOHN

Yes, I was mad. Not just at Maylee, but at Petra, too. That gun should have never been at our campsite.

ABIGAIL

John stepped forward like he'd had enough. He marched over to Maylee and his jaw was clenched so tight that it hurt to look at. His eyes were blazing. He held out his hand and said, "Give me the gun."

NOLAN

I remember John looking about ready to kill her.

[pause]

Oh, come on, it's a figure of speech.

ABIGAIL

Maylee must have been surprised at how angry John was, too, because she handed him the gun.

As soon as it was in his hands, he said, "Someone take this."

I took it from him because I was closest, then I passed it to
Nolan.

NOLAN

John says, "Someone please take the gun."

He holds it out like it's burning him. But I don't remember
anyone moving forward. Last I saw, he still had it.

JOHN

I didn't even like touching the gun. It felt oily. Slick. Ready to go
off at any moment. I handed it to Petra right away.

PETRA

John handed the gun to Abigail, who checked to make sure the
safety was on. He said, "I don't suppose you have any way to lock
that up, do you?"

I didn't.

He said, "Well, that's great, isn't it? Now I can go to sleep
knowing there's a weapon in the camp, wondering who's going
to get their hands on it next."

Maylee looked chastised for once. I told John I was sorry. I
said I shouldn't have brought it.

He said, "You're right, you shouldn't have. This is beyond
irresponsible. Someone could be *killed*. What were you thinking,

Petra?" Then he turned to Maylee and was like, "And *you*. Playing with a gun like it's a toy. What kind of charmed life do you live that you can take a risk like that? You need to get a grip. You all need to get a grip."

Then he stomped toward his tent.

ABIGAIL

Maylee was quiet for a moment. Then she glanced at Petra and actually seemed kinda solemn. She said, "Sorry."

That was it, just the one word.

NOLAN

At that point, the night is pretty much over. No one's in the mood to hang out. Maylee follows John into their tent. I say I'm going to bed, too—only I can't manage to work my tent's zipper and Petra has to help me. She says, "Sleep it off, Nolan. Good night."

PETRA

Abigail and I were left standing there alone. I could hear everyone in the other tents shuffling around, changing into pajamas. The fire was starting to die and it was getting cold.

The whole situation with the gun left me feeling sick. Especially coming on the heels of Nolan yelling at me. I was embarrassed and ashamed. I never meant to hurt anyone. And

Maylee... I hated what I'd seen in her eyes. I used to think her recklessness was fun and exciting. But suddenly it was...I don't know. Immature. Dangerous.

I wanted the night to end. I wanted the whole camping trip to end.

I looked at Abigail, and she was staring right back at me, head-on. There wasn't anything wishy-washy in her expression, not anymore. She said, "You really shouldn't have brought the gun."

I said, "I know."

I moved forward, ready to burrow deep into my sleeping bag.

Behind me I heard Abigail moving, too.

That's when I remembered she was sharing a tent with me.

27

John, you were clearly uncomfortable with the
gun. You want to tell us more about that?

JOHN

[pause]

Let's say that historically, things don't go great for Black kids
around loaded guns.

I can't look at it and see a piece of sporting equipment
or something I'd carry for protection. To me, being around a
gun is a good way to either get shot or be blamed for shooting
someone else.

And it was a *cop's* gun, of all things. It put me in a really
messed-up situation, which I didn't appreciate—especially after
last year. I'm guessing you already know about the accident?

[pause]

In my own words?

I see.

[pause]

Can I have a minute to speak to my lawyer? Privately?

[short break]

All right. This doesn't have anything to do with what happened last night, but I'll tell you my side of it.

Last year Andy Snyder—that's my best friend—and I went to a party. We both drank alcohol. Later, Andy decided to drive home, and I got in the car with him. I knew he wasn't okay to drive, but I didn't try to stop him. It didn't even occur to me.

[pause]

My parents are cautious people. Always warning me about bad things happening if I do this or that. But up until that night, the worst injury I'd had was a sprained ankle from a trampoline. My therapist says it's common for people to feel invincible if they've never been in a situation that proves otherwise. I guess that's why I got into the car with Andy. Part of me believed I was invincible.

But I wasn't. Neither of us were. Andy... He smashed the car into a tree. Which honestly might be the luckiest thing that's ever happened to us. I think all the time about how it could have been another car. What if we'd *killed* someone? How could we live with something like that?

I got banged up in the crash, but nothing permanent. Andy, though...

[pause]

Sorry.

It was a year ago, but it's still hard to talk about. One minute we were flying down the road, laughing about something that had happened in physics class the day before, the next there was screeching metal, and the smell of something burning, and my whole world turned upside down.

Andy hadn't been wearing his seat belt. When I looked at him, at first I thought he was dead. No one could bleed that much and not die. I opened the car door and started vomiting. I should have been helping Andy, but I didn't even call 911. A trucker who was on the road behind us made the call. She was the one who pulled Andy from the wreckage while I tried not to pass out.

It turned out he was alive but in a coma. I don't remember exactly how long it lasted. A week at least. Week and a half. The doctors weren't sure he'd ever come out of it.

During that week, while we were waiting to see if he lived or died, Andy's mom... She got it in her head that *I'd* been the one driving the car. She thought after the accident, I switched places with Andy so I wouldn't get in trouble.

[pause]

Andy's white, for the record.

[pause]

Your department looked into the claims. Kids who saw us leaving the party said Andy was driving and the trucker who pulled over to help confirmed it. My prints weren't on the wheel. I don't even know how to drive a manual transmission. But that wasn't enough for Mrs. Snyder.

It was Petra's dad, Lieutenant Whitfield, who sat my parents and me down to discuss the situation. He said Andy's mom was terrified. She was turning her fear into anger at me because that made it easier to cope. He said her son might die, and she was trying to let him die a hero.

Lieutenant Whitfield is usually an okay guy, but that conversation didn't sit right with me. It felt like, what, I have to accept *my* reputation being ruined, just so a white kid doesn't look like a villain?

Then Mrs. Snyder started organizing these... I don't know what to call them. Protests, I guess. She actually got a *news crew* to show up outside the hospital while a bunch of people gathered to shout about how the police hadn't arrested me.

My mom *works* at the hospital. She had to walk past those people just to do her job. Meanwhile, I was at home, still recovering from the accident, afraid my best friend would die, watching my town turn against me.

[pause]

That was when my parents found me a therapist.

And a lawyer.

My dad worried it would make me look guilty, but my mom said my whole future was on the line. Every opportunity they'd worked to give me was going to be obliterated by a white woman who wouldn't face the consequences of her son's actions. She said we weren't going to roll over and take it—and if that meant getting a lawyer involved, that's what we'd do. My mom was ready to burn the world down to protect me.

The night we hired the lawyer, my mom came into my room to say good night and ask if I needed my pain meds. I was... I guess I was feeling a lot of guilt. Lawyers aren't cheap, right? I knew my parents had a small college fund for me—not a ton of money, that's why they're so hopeful for scholarships, but a little. I told my mom they should use that to pay the lawyer. I said I'd contribute what I'd saved from tutoring, too. My mom's face crumpled, and she burst into tears. She said, "No, baby, that's *your* money. You keep it." It was the only time that week I saw her crack.

[pause]

Then Andy woke up. He came out of the coma and as soon as he could speak, he told his mom he'd been the one driving. She backed off immediately. Gave me a half-assed—I mean half-*hearted*—apology. It was basically, "I'm sorry this happened, but it was an honest mistake."

And that was it.

She'd tried to destroy my life and couldn't even look me in the eye and admit how wrong she'd been. It's like she thought everything would go right back to how it used to be. I guess for her it did—must be nice, huh? For me, even though the slander stopped, the damage was done.

How can I look at this town the same, knowing the way it turned on me? When I walk down the street or through the halls at school, now I wonder how many people would betray me without a thought. I wonder how many friends or acquaintances secretly think I'm capable of something criminal just because I'm Black. Because what happened *was* about race. Maybe that wasn't the *only* factor, but it was a big one. Mrs. Snyder doesn't see me as a full person. And since I'm not a full person, it's okay to accuse and exonerate me at her will.

I learned a lot about how the world works last year.

Nothing will go back to the way it was.

I'll never be invincible again.

[pause]

Andy and I don't hang out much anymore—not outside of school, anyway. What am I going to do, go over to his house for dinner, have a nice chat with his mom? And he's too embarrassed to come to my house. Which is for the best. My parents don't want me anywhere near him.

It makes me a little sad, but losing a friendship isn't as bad as what I could have lost. Sometimes it feels like I was this close. What if Andy had died? What if the cops hadn't asked witnesses who'd been driving the car? What if I *had* been driving?My life would be over. One second, one dumb decision, one car I shouldn't have gotten into, and everything could've been taken away.

And here's the thing: Maylee *knew* all this. She knew how precarious my future felt. She knew how bad I'd been hurt and how much I almost lost. But last night she played games with that gun anyway. There shouldn't have even *been* a gun. Why did Petra think it was okay to put me in that situation?

She *didn't* think, that's the problem. Why would she? She and Maylee are white girls from good families. They're allowed to take risks. They're allowed to make mistakes.

The fact that neither of them stopped to consider that my life doesn't work that way...it made me wonder what I was doing on that camping trip. It made me wonder why I was hanging out with them at all.

[pause]

So yes, as you put it, I was *uncomfortable* with the gun.

28

What happened after the incident with the gun?

NOLAN

I'm in my tent, feeling exhausted and wired at the same time. There's this bad feeling churning in my stomach, and I'm not sure if it's the alcohol or the entire night. So much of what happened is a blur, but I keep getting these flashes—Maylee holding the gun, Petra staring at me with a betrayed expression.

[pause]

Did Petra say anything about...I don't know. Being upset with me or something?

[pause]

Fine. I get it. You're not going to tell me what anyone else said.

Anyway, I'm lying on top of my sleeping bag, cold, but too

tired to climb into it. It feels like I'm in a hammock, like the whole ground is swaying beneath me. I can hear raised voices—Maylee and John arguing—but I don't know what they're saying.

I don't remember falling asleep. My memory just blanks out for a while.

ABIGAIL

Petra and I got into our sleeping bags. We didn't speak at all.

I wished I was at home. Or at the very least, I wished I was sleeping in my own tent. But I didn't still wish I was in Maylee's. Not anymore.

PETRA

Maylee and John were arguing. They were trying to be quiet but failing hard. Especially Maylee. What did *she* have to be mad about?

She was probably upset that someone had challenged her. That someone dared to put an end to her fun.

ABIGAIL

I felt anger rolling off Petra's skin. I thought about leaving the tent because I wasn't that tired. I could just sit by the campfire for a while. But I didn't want to be any closer to Maylee and John's fight. It was mostly *his* voice that carried across the campsite to me.

He had every right to be angry. We were *all* upset.

But still. It made me wonder if Maylee was okay. If she was safe in that tent with him.

JOHN

Did Maylee and I argue?

[pause]

My lawyer advises me not to answer that question.

NOLAN

When I wake up, the darkness inside my tent seems deeper somehow. I don't look at the time, but I know it must be late.

I roll over, try to go back to sleep, but there's a weird noise outside.

A branch snapping.

Then a piece of wood hitting a tree, two quick raps.

Rap, rap.

It moves to another tree.

Rap, rap.

Something is outside in the woods, just beyond our campsite, from the sound of it. It's circling us.

For the record, these raps I'm hearing, a lot of people in NACRO think they're a form of communication.

My mouth goes dry. My lungs feel crushed. A bigfoot is out there. I've spent the last several years afraid of and fascinated by these creatures, and now one is outside my tent.

I know I should get my camera. This is why I came on the trip. This is the whole fucking point. But now that I'm in the moment, I'm too much of a coward to even sit up, as if lying still is gonna somehow protect me.

I keep having these memories of being eleven—the way it felt when the bigfoot made eye contact with me. The malice in its expression.

And then there's a sound that freezes my blood.

Oooowhoo.

The bigfoot is calling.

ABIGAIL

An hour must have passed since we all lay down, but I was still wide awake. I doubted I'd sleep at all. Outside the tent, bugs chirped and leaves rustled. I heard an owl hoot.

JOHN

I fell asleep.

You look skeptical, but it's the truth. The entire day had been exhausting. Maylee and I both passed out.

NOLAN

It's roaming around the campsite. Getting closer.

I can almost smell it. That rotten odor that I've never forgotten. I think I can hear it breathing.

It stops right outside my tent, and I'm thinking...

Jesus, I'm ashamed to admit this. But in that moment, it's like my normal brain stops working and I only have this animal brain left, a brain that doesn't know how to do anything except fight to survive.

And my animal brain is thinking about how it's always girls that disappear around Salvation Creek. So maybe the bigfoot will leave me alone. Maybe it'll take one of them instead.

PETRA

The woods are different every time you go into them. Sometimes the forest is alive with sounds. Other nights it feels like being in a void. I know it's the weather, wind and stuff, but it seems almost like the forest has moods.

Last night, its mood was silent and watchful.

I lay in my sleeping bag for a long time after Maylee and John stopped arguing, running everything that had happened during the day through my mind. Something felt wrong, but I couldn't place what.

Then I realized it wasn't *one* wrong thing; it was a bunch of little things that added up. Maylee wanting to go camping in the first place. Her choosing Salvation Creek. Abigail being invited. Maylee's weird reaction when we found the cabin. Her being more reckless than usual. The situation with the gun.

It was a lot. When I started adding everything up, it was a whole freaking lot.

ABIGAIL

I could tell from the way Petra was breathing that she was awake, too. I didn't say anything to her. I didn't want to talk. I curled onto my side and tried to hear what was happening outside the tent.

NOLAN

I don't know how long the bigfoot is there, hovering near the entrance to my tent. When you're lying in the dark fearing for your life, it's easy to lose track of time. The creature eventually shuffles away. It makes another *oooowhoo* sound. Maybe an hour passes. I'm not sure.

PETRA

Several times during the day I'd asked Maylee what was going on, and when she said nothing, I let it go. I let it go even though I *knew* she was lying.

I needed to talk to her.

Immediately.

ABIGAIL

Petra was tossing and turning.

Then, the next thing I knew, she climbed out of her sleeping bag. I whispered, "Are you going to the bathroom?"

She said, "I'm going to talk to Maylee."

PETRA

I accidentally woke Abigail up. She asked what I was doing, and I said nothing, that I'd be right back.

She told me I should stay.

But by that point I was already out of the tent.

ABIGAIL

I didn't think she should bother Maylee. I just...I don't know. I thought we all needed a good night's sleep.

NOLAN

I'm still lying on my back, too scared to move. I hear a tent unzipping. My heart sinks. Is it John? Abigail?

No.

It's Petra.

I can tell by the way she clomps across the campsite in those big ugly boots.

I want to call out to her, tell her to get back into her tent, tell her it's not safe out there. But when I try to speak, I can't find my voice.

PETRA

I didn't want to barge in on Maylee and John, so I called out to them first. No one answered, so I spoke louder. When there was still nothing, I unzipped the tent.

JOHN

I woke up dazed, only half aware that someone was calling my name. Even in the dark, something felt off. I rubbed my eyes and was about to respond to whoever had been calling me—Petra, I thought, but wasn't sure—when the tent unzipped and a flashlight was pointed in my face.

PETRA

John looked at me with sleepy, startled eyes.

Beside him, there was an empty sleeping bag.

I said, "Where's Maylee?"

PART 2

We just received an update from the
search and rescue team. I'm sorry to be
the one to tell you this, but Maylee
Hayes has been found deceased.

PETRA

What?

No.

That's... No, I don't believe you.

NOLAN

Have we even been having the same conversation? I *know* she's
dead. The first thing I said to you was that I saw a bigfoot kill her.

PETRA

This is a tactic, right?

This is some messed-up police tactic to get us to spill
information.

ABIGAIL

Oh, Maylee.

[puts face in hands]

I knew it. When I saw John with blood on his hands, I knew he killed her. But hearing you say it makes it feel so different.

PETRA

This isn't happening.

[pause]

You're wrong. I'm sorry, but you must be wrong. It's not her. You found someone else. Has anyone identified the body?

Is my dad still at Salvation Creek? I want to talk to him. Call him on the radio and tell him to come back to town. Are you listening to me? Call him *now*.

JOHN

She...

[pause]

Do you...

[pause]

I don't know what to say.

[pause]

What are you supposed to say?

PETRA

Stop telling me to calm down.

Has anyone in the history of the world ever calmed down because someone told them to? What do you think? I'm *choosing* to be upset, and as soon as you tell me to stop, I'll flip a switch and be totally freaking serene?

God.

This is *your* fault. How long have we been here answering these questions? I could have been in the woods, helping with the search. If we would have gotten to her faster...

[pause]

I don't know.

[pause]

I could have done something. I could have...

[begins crying]

No, fuck you, I don't want a tissue. I want my best friend back.

29

Take as long as you need to
process this information. Is there
anything we can get you?

ABIGAIL

More tissues, please.

    And could you see if anyone has gotten ahold of my dad yet?

NOLAN

I don't need time to process the information. I've been process-
ing it for twelve fucking hours. What I need is for you to go
to Salvation Creek, find the creature that killed Maylee, and
destroy it.

[pause]

    Though, I wouldn't mind another soda.

JOHN

No.

There's nothing you can do for me.

[pause]

But... When can I talk to Maylee's mom? Is she here? I want to tell her... I don't know. I just want to talk to her. And Maylee's little sister. She worships Maylee. How is she going to—

[wipes eyes]

I'm sorry.

I just don't know how anyone's supposed to deal with this.

[pause]

Have you told Petra yet?

PETRA

What do I *need*?

I need this situation to go away.

I need to talk to Maylee.

I need to go back in time and change what happened yesterday.

I need to say no when Maylee suggested we go camping.

I need everything to be different.

ABIGAIL

I keep having of all these memories of Maylee. The way she'd reach over and squeeze my hand when we were walking together. The way she'd try to hide that she was teary when we watched sad movies. The way she always encouraged me to want more from my life. She used to tell me, "Never apologize for taking up space in the world."

PETRA

I was so mad at her last night. And that'll haunt me, you know? That I was angry and mean to her and now she's—

[breaks off crying]

ABIGAIL

During freshman year we did this big school picture, every grade packed together on the bleachers. Maylee was right in the middle of the crowd. There were hundreds of students surrounding her, but when you look at the picture, she's the first person you notice. And I guess it could be because of her blond hair or the sparkly shirt she was wearing. But I kinda think not. I think there was something about Maylee that glowed.

NOLAN

You want to know what's been on my mind the most?

Last night, I lay in my tent for...how long? An hour or something? Just lay there and listened to the bigfoot move around the campsite. If I had shouted or run out of the tent or done *anything*, maybe Maylee would still be alive.

Because that's when it must've taken her, right? When I heard the bigfoot sniffing around my tent, it was looking for Maylee. Trying to catch her scent or something. Maybe it had seen her earlier in the woods. Maybe it had marked her.

While I was lying there, too much of an asshole to do anything, the bigfoot opened her tent. It took her into the woods and killed her.

What if I could have stopped it?

JOHN

Maylee once said, "What's the point of living if you don't live big?" And she did. Always. She was so alive that she made *me* more alive by being around her.

PETRA

A couple years ago I was helping with a SAR where we already knew the missing woman was dead. She'd been lost in the wilderness for weeks, so there wasn't any hope. Still, the police were doing their best to recover her body. They wanted to give her family some sort of resolution.

One day I had a conversation with her husband. He told me the worst part was the forgetting. Already, after only a few weeks, people were forgetting the details of who his wife had been.

It's going to be that way for Maylee, isn't it? We'll remember all the big things about her, but details will vanish.

Like how her French braids were always perfect.

And how she'd sing along with the radio and laugh when she couldn't hit the high notes.

Or how she owned twenty different shades of red lipstick.

How she loved scary movies, especially the really low-budget ones.

How she could eat an entire bag of Tootsie Rolls in one sitting.

How she never read the books for English class but somehow managed to talk like she knew every word of them.

How she smelled like roses.

How she loved turtles.

How her smile could make you feel like someone was seeing you, really seeing you, appreciating you despite all your flaws.

Everything that made her a person, every pointless, useless detail will go away. She'll just be one more girl who got lost in the woods. No one will know what she added to the world.

JOHN

I'll never meet anyone like her again. Maylee is special.

ABIGAIL

I wish I could tell her how special she was. But I think she already knew. I think even she could see the way she sparkled.

PETRA

I don't think you understand. I don't know how to exist without Maylee.

NOLAN

It was right there. The bigfoot was *right* there.

PETRA

Actually, there *is* something you can do for me.

I'm sure you've got some big plan about how you're giving out information, trying to catch one of us in a lie or whatever. But...can you tell me how Maylee died?

Please?

30

Maylee's body was found five miles from
your campsite, in a crevice between
two boulders. She'd suffered bleeding from a bullet wound in her shoulder.

PETRA

Oh my God.

JOHN

She was in a crevice?

ABIGAIL

Are you saying...John tried to hide the body?

NOLAN

What? No. That can't be right. A bullet wound?

31

Let us know when you're ready to
get back to our interview.

ABIGAIL

I'm ready. Or as ready as I can be. I'm not any less ready than I
was when we first came here, which I guess wasn't *that* ready.
But what I mean is, nothing has really changed since then.

So, yes, go ahead.

JOHN

Let's just get this over with.

NOLAN

I don't know what else I could possibly tell you.

PETRA

One more thing, okay? This gunshot wound, is there any chance
it was self-inflicted?

[pause]

No. I didn't think it was.

[pause]

So you're telling me that Maylee was shot. Someone *shot* her. Maylee isn't just dead, she was *murdered*.

That's what you're saying, right?

[pause]

Okay. Go ahead. Ask your questions. Let's catch the monster who did this.

32

When we left off, Petra had just discovered that Maylee wasn't in her tent.

JOHN

I didn't realize I was alone until Petra shined her light on the
spot where Maylee should've been sleeping. At first, I was only
confused.

PETRA

I instantly knew something bad had happened.

[pause]

Don't look at me like that. I'm not just saying this in hindsight,
okay? As soon as I saw Maylee was gone, I felt sick. I asked John
where she'd gone, and he rubbed his eyes and said, "I thought
she was right here."

I turned and shined my light around the rest of the campsite, but there was no sign of her. That's when I shouted for Nolan and Abigail to wake up.

ABIGAIL

I was already putting my boots on when Petra yelled for me. She said to get up. She said Maylee was missing.

NOLAN

A few seconds after I hear Petra moving around the campsite, she shouts that Maylee is gone. My heart sinks. I knew the bigfoot got her.

[pause]

Are you *sure* about her getting shot?

Well, maybe... I don't know. Have you ever seen a situation where an animal bite could look like a bullet wound?

PETRA

Everyone crawled out of their tents. We stood in the middle of the campsite, around the glowing embers of the campfire. I said, "Maylee is missing."

I expected someone to say something like, "What do you mean, she's *missing*?"

But they didn't.

The three of them stared at me like I was giving them old news.

ABIGAIL

It was... I don't know. It was a tense situation. I said, "Maybe she went to the bathroom."

PETRA

Maylee hadn't just gone to the bathroom—her phone was lying on her pillow.

Abigail was like, "What's that have to do with it?"

Um, did she know Maylee at all? John jumped in and said, "Maylee doesn't go *anywhere* without her phone."

Even though we had no signal, she wouldn't have risked missing a photo op. Like, Maylee literally only buys pants with pockets because she can't bear not having her phone physically on her.

Nolan said, "Seriously? Her phone is here?"

I was like, oh good, he agrees that this is concerning.

But then he said, "That's one of the commonalities. All these forest disappearances happen when people don't have their phone on them."

And I said—well, okay, I was kind of shouting, "Are you kidding me right now? *Obviously* people not having a phone increases their chances of disappearing. Otherwise, they'd call someone and say, 'Hey, I'm lost, please find me.' God, Nolan, it's scarier if someone disappears *with* their phone."

I swear, his NACRO crap destroyed his ability to think critically.

JOHN

I told everyone that fighting wasn't going to solve anything. We needed to focus on the problem. Petra agreed. She held up her phone and said, "We'll set a timer for five minutes. If Maylee's not back by then, we'll go look for her. In the meantime, let's come up with a plan."

NOLAN

There's a bloodthirsty bigfoot raging through the woods and Petra wants to *make a plan*.

PETRA

I had everyone's attention, so I asked, "Can anyone think of why Maylee would go into the forest?"

Nolan said, "Who says she had a choice?"

John gave him a weird look and asked what he was talking about.

And do you know what Nolan said? Do you know what he actually had the nerve to say? He said, "It was a bigfoot."

The worst part is, I think he really believed it.

JOHN

I was half-asleep when we realized Maylee was missing. I think that's why I wasn't more immediately concerned. It wasn't until Nolan commented that Maylee might have been taken against her will—and I thought of how *watched* I felt earlier—that the gravity of the situation hit me.

NOLAN

Petra straight up blows off the fact that I heard something moving around the campsite. John's giving me this baffled look like he can't even comprehend what I'm saying. But I notice the expression on Abigail's face. The fear in her eyes. *She* believes me. When the bigfoot was prowling around our campsite, I think maybe she heard it, too.

PETRA

Next, John started in. He said, "I told you I felt like someone was out here with us. Not a creature but a person, whoever owns that cabin. Maybe they—"

I cut him off. I reminded him that the chances of some human predator being at Salvation Creek were practically zero.

[pause]

Which shows how much I know. John was right after all. There *was* a killer in the woods. Only they weren't hiding in the trees watching us; they were standing there at the fire.

Right?

Isn't that what you think?

[pause]

Can you answer a question for once? My best friend is *dead*, and I don't know why. Do you even have a clue what that feels like? Are you on some freaking power trip? Does it make you feel big to withhold information from a—

[pause]

No, I don't need to *take a break*.

I need answers. Who do you think shot Maylee? *Who?* Stop looking at me like that and answer my fucking question!

[long pause]

Yes, I'm fine to continue. I'm sorry I knocked over the coffee.

Where had I been?

Right.

I asked John about his fight with Maylee.

JOHN

No, I didn't consider that any of us had hurt Maylee. I *still* haven't considered it. I trust everyone who was on the camping trip.

ABIGAIL

John was the last person to see Maylee alive. We *know* they were in the tent together. Now she's dead. Even if I hadn't seen blood on him, wouldn't that be suspicious?

NOLAN

I ask them if they'd heard the animal call. The *oooowhoo* sound. If they'd heard the sticks breaking. If they'd heard rapping on trees.

No one responds.

PETRA

John said yes, they'd fought. He was mad about the gun. Maylee was mad that *he* was mad. She accused him of being boring and ruining all her fun.

I asked, "Was she really upset or Maylee-upset?"

John looked like he didn't understand what I was talking about.

So I said, "Really upset is...you know. Genuine hurt. Agitation. And Maylee-upset is when she acts unhappy because that's what feels interesting in the moment."

I glanced around the group and they were all staring at me like I was pure evil. John said, "Petra... You don't really believe that about her, do you?"

That's when I realized I was the only one there who truly knew Maylee at all.

JOHN

It wasn't the first time Maylee's been accused of being manipulative. But I never expected to hear it from Petra.

ABIGAIL

Petra was asking John all these rapid questions, like she was a TV detective or something. I felt bad for him because at that moment, I was sure he hadn't done anything to Maylee. Which makes me cringe now, thinking about how wrong I was.

PETRA

I asked John how he and Maylee had ended the conversation. He said, "We were cool. She apologized for firing the gun. I apologized for raising my voice."

I asked, "And then what?"

John said, "Nothing. We went to sleep."

I asked, "Did she use her skin cream first?"

John looked at me blankly, which I took as a no.

Look, it might seem silly to you, but before years of trying different products and a billion visits to the dermatologist, Maylee's acne was pretty bad. I think her biggest fear in life was it coming back. Personally, I'm all for normalizing influencers with freaking skin texture, but Maylee thought it would ruin her whole career.

My point is this: Even if she was thrown off by the alcohol and the fight and camping in general, I couldn't buy that she'd gone to sleep without doing her skin-care ritual. Which meant she hadn't been planning on going to sleep.

All I said to the group was, "That's interesting."

John asked why.

Before I could answer, the timer on my phone went off.

NOLAN

Abigail says, "Maybe we should wait five more minutes?" Surprisingly, Petra agrees. She resets the timer.

I really don't want these five minutes to pass—because when they do, Petra is gonna demand that we go into the woods after Maylee. I have no desire to go into the woods. Not in the dark. Not without protection.

What I *actually* want is for us to leave. I'm sorry to say that—and it's especially messed up now, knowing what happened. But at the moment, I'm thinking let's just get out of here. Forget

Maylee; let's get in the car and bolt. I thought I wanted to find a bigfoot, prove they were real, but now that I'm in the situation, I only want to flee.

So I say, "Maybe you guys should wait here for Maylee while I drive until I have service and call for help."

Petra scowls and says, "You're drunk, Nolan. You're not driving anywhere. And we don't need help."

PETRA

I couldn't let myself believe we needed help. Getting help would mean the situation had already spiraled out of our control.

Maylee hadn't been gone for long. It was absurd to think we should be calling the police already. We'd wait for her to come back, or we'd go find her and all have a laugh about it.

[pause]

You never know when you're entering a survival situation.

ABIGAIL

The timer on Petra's phone went off again.

Ten minutes had passed.

Maylee wasn't back.

33

At that point you decided to
search for Maylee?

JOHN

Petra made that decision for all of us. Personally, I wanted to call
the police.

[pause]

Yes, I know that earlier I wanted to avoid law enforcement.
That was before my girlfriend was missing in the woods.

PETRA

I told everyone we needed to stick together. The worst thing we
could do at that moment was split up.

NOLAN

Yeah, no shit. What, we're gonna separate and let the bigfoot
pick us off one by one?

JOHN

Except what would happen if we all left the campsite and Maylee came back to find it abandoned?

PETRA

John made a good point—that someone needed to stay in case Maylee came back. I still thought that was likely. I mean, I certainly wasn't entertaining the possibility that we were in a life-and-death—

[pause]

Sorry. I just keep forgetting. It's easy to talk about until I remember how it ended.

[pause]

Anyway. John was right. So I said Nolan and I would look for Maylee while Abigail and John waited at camp.

NOLAN

I'm like, gee, thanks for volunteering me for the more deadly task, sis.

PETRA

I asked Nolan if he was really going to complain right then—*really*?

ABIGAIL

I told Petra I'd go look for Maylee with her. I wasn't scared. I'm more comfortable in the woods than Nolan, anyhow.

Petra said, "That's why I need you to stay here. John and Nolan don't know how to handle the wilderness."

Gosh, this might sound silly, but Petra saying that made me really happy. She thought I was competent, which is probably the highest praise someone can get from her.

PETRA

Abigail had to stay at the campsite, because God forbid we need to start another fire, or make an informed decision or something. She was the only other person in the group with...

[pause]

Hold on. I'm thinking.

[pause]

Why *did* Abigail want to go into the woods? I thought she was trying to keep the peace. But maybe she specifically wanted to look for Maylee. After all...

What you said about them dating before, that was true, wasn't it? You're not using some tactic on me?

Okay.

So Abigail and Maylee used to date.

And Abigail is still hung up on Maylee, clearly, with no signs that the feelings are reciprocated. Then Abigail offers to go into the woods to look for her. And we already know Papa Hillbilly Supreme taught her how to shoot.

[pause]

I'm not saying *anything* right now. Just thinking all of that is pretty interesting.

JOHN

I didn't want anything to do with the woods at night. I hadn't even wanted to hike when the *sun* was out.

But Maylee's my girlfriend.

[pause]

Was my girlfriend.

She needed me, and I wasn't going to let her down.

I told Petra *I* would go into the forest with her.

NOLAN

Abigail keeps saying, "Are you sure this is a good idea? Maybe we should wait just a little bit longer? I'm sure Maylee's fine."

But you've been talking to Petra for a while now. I'm sure

you realize that when she gets something in her head, nothing is gonna change her mind.

ABIGAIL

I was okay with them going to look for Maylee. Why wouldn't I be okay with it? That doesn't even make sense. Same as everyone else, I just wanted Maylee to be found.

PETRA

So that settled it.

John and I would go into the woods.

Nolan and Abigail would wait at camp.

I passed out flashlights to everyone. I handed John a bottle of water and told him he should put a jacket over his sweatshirt unless he wanted to get sick. He shrugged me off, said he never gets colds. I was like, "Whatever. Don't complain to me later."

He nodded, but the way he was pacing back and forth and glancing nervously into the woods, I'm not sure he was even paying attention.

I grabbed my hiking backpack. It had my compass, granola bars, extra batteries, a first aid kit, a flare. Everything I could possibly need. Just because I was venturing into the woods at night, didn't mean I wasn't doing it *smartly*.

Then I told the group that John and I would search for

Maylee for exactly one hour. If she hadn't turned up by then, we'd go to the police.

[pause]

Yes, of course I realize we didn't end up here until early this morning. God. Isn't it obvious by now that things didn't go according to plan?

34

What happened when you went into the woods?

PETRA

You know what's messed up?

Maylee's death has changed everything.

I can't tell you what happened when John and I went into the woods in the same way I would've told you a few hours ago.

Because now I'm thinking back about it differently. I'm trying to remember everything John said to me. I'm wondering if I went into the forest with a killer.

JOHN

Petra and I hiked down the same hill from earlier and headed toward the creek. I hoped she knew where she was going, because the shadows were disorienting.

PETRA

At the time, I wasn't afraid to be alone with John. If anything, *he* was the one who was acting scared, shining his flashlight back and forth so fast it was making me dizzy. At one point something rustled in the brush and I swear he jumped about a foot.

I was like, "It's going to be a long night if you freak out about every forest noise."

John said, "It's already been a long night."

JOHN

It was dark. Our flashlights didn't illuminate much. I wouldn't say I was *scared*—not yet. But I was uncomfortable. Even more so when Petra started shouting.

PETRA

I called Maylee's name and John was like, "What are you doing?" He had this look of horror on his face.

What did he expect? What if Maylee *had* just gone to the bathroom and tripped over a rock and sprained her ankle? In SAR training we learned how frequently a person becomes incapacitated without falling unconscious. *Of course* I was going to shout for Maylee to see if she'd shout back.

But John was looking at me with wide, panicky eyes. He said, "What if someone else hears us? What if someone else *answers*?"

JOHN

My thought process is, you're in a situation where you don't know who's nearby and what their intentions are; don't go around screaming and reveal your location.

PETRA

I kept shouting for Maylee, obviously. What, was I supposed to let John's paranoia influence my decisions?

35

What happened after Petra and
John went into the woods?

ABIGAIL

A few minutes after they went down the hill, we heard Petra
shouting for Maylee.

NOLAN

She probably wakes up everything in a fifty-mile radius with the
way she's shouting. I'm sitting there thinking, "Well, great, she's
gonna summon the bigfoot right to us."

ABIGAIL

Nolan's gaze was darting around the clearing like he thought we
were surrounded. I asked if he was okay, and he said yes. It was
definitely a lie. I told him, "I don't think there are any bigfoots
around."

He said, "I heard it. About an hour, maybe two hours, before Petra got us up, I heard it moving around the campsite."

I don't know if I've ever seen anyone so scared as he was right then. He was shaking, you know? I felt super guilty, which was why I said, "You probably heard Maylee."

He frowned and said, "What?"

I told him, "When you heard the creature moving around the campsite, that was probably Maylee leaving."

He sat back and thought about it for a second. Then he said. "I don't think so. It was big. And I heard the way it was breathing. It couldn't have been human."

NOLAN

I ask Abigail what *she* thinks happened to Maylee. She looks away and says, "I don't know. I guess maybe she went for a walk?"

Maylee went for a stroll in the middle of the night? Yeah, sure, sounds legit.

We're quiet for a while. The woods buzz with sound: insects chirping and rustling bushes, branches scratching against each other in the breeze. The campfire is hardly burning anymore but still gives off some heat. In the distance Petra shouts for Maylee, but her voice is more remote now. It feels like she and John are in another world.

I don't know what makes me say it, maybe just the strangeness of the whole night, but I'm like, "You care about Maylee a lot, don't you?"

Abigail hesitates. Then she nods.

I ask, "Do you love her?"

Another long pause, then she says, "I used to. I thought I'd stopped, but maybe you can't ever really stop loving someone once you start. What do you think?"

I tell her I don't know; I've never been in love.

Abigail says, "It'll happen eventually."

She says it like she's sure of it, which I like. We're silent for another moment, then the next words pour from my mouth before I even know I'm gonna say them. I'm like, "This might be weird but...there's no chance that you and I..."

I'm not even finished before Abigail starts shaking her head. She says, "No. There's no chance. I'm sorry."

I shrug and say, "Didn't think so, but I thought I'd check."

It's not wrong to *ask*, right?

Abigail gets kind of weird, though. Guarded or something. She's like, "Are you going to be less nice to me now?"

I'm genuinely confused. Like, does she think I've only been nice to her to get in her pants or something? I tell her, "Of course not. I think you're really cool. I'd like to be friends."

ABIGAIL

Until recently, Maylee and I hadn't hung out for a long time. Just about a year. But one day, after she came back into my life, we were sitting on her back patio, talking. It was actually the first time I'd been to her house, and it was so much bigger and nicer than I'd imagined. Like something from a magazine.

Do you ever look at pictures of magazine houses and think no one could actually *live* like that? Those places must be like movie sets, designed just for show. But gosh, when I went to Maylee's house I saw—

[pause]

Right. Sorry. I'll focus.

We were on the back patio, and Maylee said, "We're friends, aren't we, Abigail?"

I nodded without really thinking about it. Maylee said we were friends, so that was it: we were. But later, when I thought about it more, I guess I kinda wondered...if we were friends, where had she been for the past year? Why was it so easy for her to stop talking to me? Why did she only come back when she wanted something?

It was way different when Nolan mentioned being friends. I know he was still drunk because of the way he slurred his words, so maybe I should forget everything he said last night. But for some reason, when he made that comment, I don't know...it felt really sincere. Like over the past day, something between us had actually really clicked.

36

Did you see any sign of Maylee in the woods?

PETRA

No.

Nothing.

But you need to remember that it was, I don't know, one in the morning? The moon was nearly full, but it had been behind clouds for most of the night. We had flashlights, but they didn't exactly light up the whole forest.

It's easy to miss things out there. Really easy. We could have been trampling right over Maylee's footprints and never known it.

JOHN

It was dark and cold. Petra was getting more worried by the moment—which made *me* more worried. I kept thinking about the footprint Nolan had found. How someone might have been at our camp shortly before we got there. How they easily they might have come back.

PETRA

We walked along the creek, swinging our flashlights back and forth and calling Maylee's name. At least, *I* called her. John was still too afraid to make any noise. Every few minutes I stopped and listened for Maylee, but she never shouted back. The forest was strangely quiet.

Something was nagging at me, though I couldn't figure out what. Some detail I couldn't grasp. I kept thinking that I was sure Maylee hadn't gone to sleep, and I was sure she'd walked away from the campsite of her own volition. But *why*?

JOHN

I thought of the story I'd seen in Maylee's notebook. The one about a girl who's lost in the woods. I don't believe in premonitions, and I don't think Maylee could have foreseen what happened last night.

But the thought was unnerving.

PETRA

We moved farther from the campsite, following the same route we had earlier in the day. That's when it clicked—a small piece of the puzzle, at least: we were on a path Maylee already knew.

JOHN

Out of nowhere, Petra stopped. I plowed into her, almost knocked myself down. She spun around to face me and said, "The cabin. John, *the cabin*."

I saw how excited she was. But personally, just hearing her mention that place made me feel sick to my stomach.

PETRA

I knew beyond a doubt that I'd find Maylee at the cabin. I'd never been so sure of anything in my life. And yet John was already shaking his head, saying, "We can't go there."

Excuse me? Did he want to find Maylee or not?

Since he's generally a very reasonable guy, I tried using logic. I was like, "What if Maylee got hurt walking around the woods and went to the cabin because it was the closest shelter she knew of?"

I immediately saw that he wasn't swayed. He said, "Petra, I'm telling you, that place is *dangerous*. If Maylee's there... If she's there, then we've got a big problem, because I don't think she's alone."

I clenched my fists and tried to keep my voice even as I said, "Okay, then. Why don't you come up with a better plan?"

He didn't even have to think about it. He said, "We find a place we have cell service and call the police. We let *them* search the shack."

He was serious. He was actually freaking serious.

I was thinking, hold up a second. He didn't want to go to the cabin because he thought some psychopath had Maylee captive, or whatever his theory was. Yet he was willing to waste precious minutes while we waited for the police to show?

How long would that even take? We'd have to hike back to the campsite, get everyone in the car, drive until our phones worked, wait for the police to show up, lead them through the woods...

I said, "And do you know what happens in that *several-hour* window when this is all going down? Maylee *dies*."

[pause]

At the time, as I was saying all that, I was trying to convey urgency to John. But the truth is, it never felt *that* critical. I never actually thought Maylee might—

[pause]

Oh God, how can she be dead?

JOHN

I kept picturing those knives on the wall. Hanging there, sharp and sinister, waiting for their owner to come home.

I didn't want to go to the shack—just like I hadn't wanted to go earlier. I hadn't wanted to hike. I hadn't wanted to chase Nolan through the woods. I hadn't wanted to go camping in the first place. I was tired and scared and sick of people making decisions for me.

So I pointed to a big rock and said, "Do what you have to, but I'm waiting here."

PETRA

I told John no. It wasn't safe to split up.

And he...kinda snapped. He stepped toward me and said, "I don't *want* to split up. I want us to call the police instead of busting into that shack like we're playing action hero. But you're unwilling to listen to reason—you're unwilling to listen to *any* plan that you didn't come up with. And I'm done with that."

[pause]

Well, *yes*, I saw his point.

What was I supposed to do, though, abandon Maylee? I told John, "I'm going to the cabin."

I assumed he was bluffing. That he'd cave when he realized

I wasn't going to. But he didn't. He sat down on the rock and said, "Fine."

So that was that.

I'd go the rest of the way alone.

I was about to walk away when John said, "Petra?"

I turned back.

He was holding his flashlight in shaky hands, glancing into the shadows between trees. I thought he might make one last plea for me to stay or maybe even get in a parting shot. But he said, "Be safe."

It made me...I don't know. I guess I teared up a little. I was scared. Probably the most scared I'd ever been. I told John to be safe, too.

Then I walked toward the cabin.

37

What was happening at the campsite?

NOLAN

It feels like an eternity has passed since Petra left. It feels like enough time for her to go into the forest, be stalked by a bigfoot, get eaten, and for the still-hungry bigfoot to return to our camp.

Abigail and I huddle around the burned-out fire. It's fucking freezing, and I'm thinking about starting it up again, because who knows how long we'll be waiting, but I've always been shit at making fires. Like, I'd probably go through all the kindling we have left before succeeding. I could ask Abigail to help, but I just can't bring myself to admit that I'm basically useless.

Besides, for all I know, flames might attract the bigfoot to our camp—there's mixed data on how they react to fire.

Abigail doesn't seem bothered by the cold. She's distracted, sitting all hunched into herself and biting her nails.

That's when I realize... I don't know. I've been so stuck in my own head. As soon as I heard the creature moving around camp, that survival instinct started up in me. I've only been thinking about myself.

When some people are in a crisis, they spring to action. A screwed-up situation like the one we're in—one of us lost, something malevolent lurking in the woods—this is what shows who you truly are. Some people step up and prove themselves. Some people find out they have a deep well of bravery inside of them.

Then there are people like me.

How can I be so concerned about my own safety when my *sister* is out there? Because the thing is, I love Petra.

Yeah, yeah. All I've done is complain about her all day—Day? Is it still day? You can see how frustrating she is. She's basically impossible to be around. But in the end, that doesn't matter, because Petra is family. And I let her go into the woods. I *knew* something that could *kill* her was out there, and I let her go anyway. For the first time, I wonder what I'll do if she doesn't come back.

I'm about to raise my concerns to Abigail, but she suddenly stands up and says, "I think I should go after Petra and John."

It's basically what I was thinking, so I say, "I'll go."

Abigail's startled. She wasn't expecting me to go with her. That's how much of a coward she thinks I am.

When she replies, it's in mumbles, all, "Um, no, that's okay. I was just going to... I won't go far or anything."

I interrupt her and say, "I can do this." I start to stand up but move too fast and the whole world seesaws. I sit down hard and wait for the dizziness to pass.

Abigail says, "I really think it should be me."

I tell her, "I swear, I can handle it. I won't run away if things get intense."

She bites her lip. She's thinking and thinking, and every second, my shame grows. Finally, she says, "You've been drinking."

I point out that she has been, too.

She's like, "Not the way you were."

And okay, she's got a point. The world does seem blurred around the edges and my brain is working a little slow. Still, I tell her, "I feel completely sober. I wasn't that drunk to start with."

Abigail says, "But..." She thinks for another long moment. Then she says, "The car!"

The car? What about it?

She's like, "You know how to drive it, right? Isn't it a manual?"

I'm like, "Yeah, so?"

She says, "I can't drive stick. If something happens, we need to be ready to go right away. That means we need someone who can drive a manual waiting here at camp."

What she's saying, it makes sense. Enough sense, anyway. So I give in and say, "Okay, sure. I'll wait here."

But the whole time I'm wondering...am I really doing it because it's the smart thing? Or is the scared animal part of my brain trying to *convince* me it's right? The decision has been made, though. I hand Abigail a flashlight. I tell her not to go too far. I tell her to be careful.

I watch as she leaves the campsite, her flashlight beam dancing in front of her. She disappears down the hill, darkness swallowing her.

Then I'm alone.

38

What happened at the cabin?

PETRA

Shadows pooled around every tree, and the air felt thicker, wetter. A storm was coming. I listened for movement, but the woods were still weirdly silent. You'd think it would be scarier to hear an animal moving around in the brush, make me afraid that something was hunting me, but that's not how it was. The quiet felt unnatural. Where were the crickets? Where was the wind? Even the flowing creek water sounded like someone had turned down the volume. I could hear the pounding of my own heart.

[pause]

No.

I didn't consider turning back.

Not for a second.

After a little while, I got to the place where we'd crossed Salvation Creek earlier that day—those mossy rocks where I'd—

[clears throat]

Sorry.

Where I'd been afraid someone was going to slip.

[pause]

Anyway, I almost missed the exact spot. Darkness warped everything. The woods at night aren't the same as the woods during the day, okay? Even if you think you know an area, you might go there after sundown and find out it's become a totally different place.

From the corner of my eye, I glimpsed a low-hanging branch covered in old-man's beard—that's a type of lichen, if you don't know. I remembered ducking under it earlier. Sure enough, when I shined my light at the creek, I saw the rocks we'd used to cross.

I was glad I had my boots on, because crossing Salvation Creek was even more precarious in the dark. The water seemed to be flowing faster, more dangerously. Once I was on the other side, I started moving through the forest. Earlier I remembered only walking a short distance before the brush cleared and we were on the trail. But last night I kept walking and walking over rough terrain. Too much time passed. I should have reached the trail faster.

Had I screwed up? Earlier in the day, on the way to the cabin the first time, had we made a turn I was forgetting? Had we passed some sort of landmark that I'd missed in the dark?

I stopped. My heart pounded. What if I'd gone too far and overshot my target? What if, thanks to my low visibility, I'd been veering to the right or left the entire time? What if I was already well beyond the trail, heading farther and farther into the woods, the cabin at my back?

I turned around and looked at where I'd come from.

I looked right and left.

I fumbled in my backpack for the compass. It wasn't in the pocket where I normally kept it. I knelt and started pulling things out, shining my light inside. The compass wasn't there. For all my talk of being prepared, I'd ended up deep in the woods with no way to tell if I was going remotely in the right direction.

That's when I heard something move. Something *close*. A crunching sound, a foot snapping twigs. I shot to my feet and looked around, but it was too dark and the trees were too dense. I couldn't see anything...but that didn't mean something couldn't see *me*. Sweat broke out on my forehead despite the cold. I started to wonder if I should've taken John's fears more seriously. And what about Maylee? I'd assumed she'd been messing with

John, feeding his fear for kicks, but what if she'd really heard noises, too?

I needed to move. I couldn't stand around waiting for...I didn't know what. I wondered if I should turn around, backtrack to the creek and start out again, pay more attention this time. Or no... Off to the left, did I remember that tree from earlier? Should I try walking that way for a few yards?

The whole time, my brain was screaming, "No, no. This is how people walk in circles. This is how people end up dying a mile from their campsite."

It felt like any choice would be wrong. Actually, I started to worry that I'd *already* made the wrong choice—that I'd made it without even realizing a choice had been made.

My heart beat rapidly, and I was having trouble catching my breath. I was starting to panic. It was important that I recognized that. Panic is okay. Panic is a normal reaction. But you need to understand when it's happening or it could lead to erratic decision-making. I had to let the panic run its course and stay still until I got a grip on myself.

I closed my eyes and counted to ten. I tried not to think of how watched I felt, how anything could be creeping closer and closer, reaching out to wrap their hand around me...

A minute later, I opened my eyes and looked around the forest again. I decided I'd been doubting myself for no reason.

The original direction I'd been heading was correct, I just misremembered how long it took to connect with the trail. And there was definitely nothing in the forest watching me.

I'd walk for two more minutes. If I didn't find the trail, I'd turn back.

And yes, I knew how risky that was. But what choice did I have?

I started walking.

Fifteen seconds passed.

I tripped over a tree root and would have probably twisted my ankle if I weren't wearing boots with excellent ankle support.

Thirty seconds.

From somewhere off in the distance came the rumble of thunder, and I tried not to think too much about it because there wasn't enough room in my brain for another worry to wedge its way in.

One minute.

Maybe I really *was* heading in the wrong direction. I told myself that no matter what happened, I should be able to find my way back to the creek. As long as I could get back to the creek, I could follow it to the campsite.

At a minute and a half, I stepped out of the trees and onto the trail.

My relief was so strong that for a moment my knees buckled.

I let out a big whoosh of breath. It was okay. Everything was okay. I had found the trail, exactly where I'd thought it would be. I was never really in danger.

Except no.

Everything *wasn't* okay.

I was so distracted by nearly getting lost that for a moment I'd forgotten what I was doing in the first place. I needed to find Maylee. I started walking quickly, almost running. How much time had I wasted?

There were no incidents once I was on the trail. It wasn't long before I spotted the cabin through the trees. For a moment, the sight of it stopped me in my tracks.

Because coming from the grimy windows, I saw a yellow glow.

Someone was inside.

39

What happened after you and Petra split up?

JOHN

At first, I did exactly what I'd said—I waited.

But the longer I was out there, the more I doubted myself. Why was I sitting around doing nothing when Maylee was lost?

[pause]

What? No, I wasn't considering following Petra. I was thinking about hiking back to camp on my own, finding a way to call the authorities.

Ten minutes probably passed. Twenty. Twenty minutes that I wasted.

I stood up.

The forest seemed larger and deeper than during the day, but I was pretty sure I could find my way through it. Then I'd just need to get the car keys—assuming Petra didn't have them—and I could try to find cell service.

I'd just started walking when I heard something moving along the creek toward me.

I froze.

It was a person.

[pause]

Yes, I'm sure.

I knew because they were trying to be quiet.

Anyone trying to be silent in the woods at two in the morning can't have good intentions.

40

When you saw lights in the cabin, did
you immediately assume it was Maylee?

PETRA

I *knew* it was Maylee.

Still, it's important to stay alert and cautious, no matter how sure you feel about a situation. I hadn't forgotten about the fresh firewood in the cabin or the jacket hanging near the door waiting for someone to come back and slip it on. If the person inside *wasn't* Maylee, they were almost certainly a hunter—meaning they'd be armed. The last thing I wanted was for them to hear me coming, get spooked, and fire a shot into the forest.

But I never thought the cabin might, like, belong to some homicidal ax murderer, if that's what you're asking. No serial killer hangs out in the woods *hoping* a victim will come along. On the other hand, my dad says most criminals are opportunists, not masterminds. So who knows.

At any rate, I approached carefully. Stealthily, I guess. I figured I'd peek through the windows, check the situation out. But they were covered with a summer's worth of grime. I tried to look in but couldn't make out anything besides the glow of lantern light.

I debated what to do.

It had to be one thirty by that point. Late but not late enough that I could wait until dawn to knock on the door—no matter how much I would have rather done it in sunlight. I needed to confirm that Maylee was inside right away. Because if she *wasn't*, then she was still in the forest somewhere and I'd have to keep looking for her.

So I knocked.

It felt like a lifetime before the cabin door swung open.

Maylee stood there, as casual as if she were lounging in her room, not inexplicably in a random cabin in the middle of the night. She looked at me for a long moment and said, "Well, shit."

I was like, "Is that all you have to say?"

She thought about it, then, I kid you not, she actually said, "Since you're here anyway, you can get the fire going. I've been trying for an hour."

41

What happened after Abigail left the campsite?

NOLAN

You know what I didn't sign up for when I agreed to go on the trip? Being alone in the woods while a murderous bigfoot stalks me.

I'm shaking.

I keep telling myself that I'm shaking from the cold, but the truth is, I'm terrified. Every sound makes me jump. I hear something that might be a howl.

I have a camping lantern blazing but realize I'm making myself a beacon. So I turn it off. Only then I can't see anything at all. And evidence points to bigfoots being nocturnal, so they have better night vision than me anyway. By turning off the lantern, I'm probably only hurting myself.

So I turn it back on.

I check how much time has passed.

I pace back and forth a few times but somehow trip over one of the camp chairs. The rapid movement of trying to right myself makes me feel like I might puke, so I sit down again. I wait longer.

All the while, I feel something watching me.

42

Did Maylee offer an explanation for being at the cabin?

PETRA

If I tell you this next part, you better use it to help find Maylee's
killer, okay? I'm doing my part, so do *yours*.

[pause]

Maylee let me into the cabin. She had a blue beanie pulled
over her hair and a flannel blanket wrapped around her shoulders. In the light of the camping lanterns, she looked like a freaking L.L.Bean ad or something. Without saying anything, I went
to the woodstove and checked out her attempts at a fire. She'd
been trying to light it without any tinder. There was a rolled-up
newspaper on the floor by the nightstand, so I pulled out a few
sheets and wedged them under the logs.

While I worked, Maylee plopped down on the cot and said, "You're not supposed to be here."

I was like, "Excuse me? *I'm* not supposed to be here? Maybe let's talk about what *you're* doing."

She reached over into the nightstand drawer, and, I can't even believe this, she took out a Tootsie Roll. Like she had a whole freaking stash in there. She said, "Want one?"

I said no, I did not. I wanted to know what the crap was going on.

She was like, "It's kind of a funny story."

I told her I bet it really wasn't.

A minute later the fire caught. I adjusted the damper, then sat at the rickety wooden table. There was a purple clay vase sitting in the middle of it, made by someone's kid, probably. I remember doing a craft just like it when I was in third grade or so.

I asked Maylee, "Whose cabin is this?"

She said, "I don't know. Some hunter."

I looked at her for a long moment, then asked if she planned to tell me what she was doing there. She unwrapped another Tootsie Roll and tossed the wrapper onto the cot. I waited. And waited. Finally, she said, "I needed to get away."

I was like, "Get away? Maylee, we're an hour from town, deep in the woods. How much more away could you be?"

She shook her head and said, "Not from town, Petra. From you. From all of you."

I was about to ask why she needed to get away from me. Of all people, why would she ever want to get away from *me*? But before I could say anything, she spoke again. She said, "Maybe I was trying to get away from myself."

Look, I'll talk forever about camping or whatever. But I'm not a heart-to-heart person. To buy myself a second to think, I reached into the open nightstand drawer and took one of Maylee's Tootsie Rolls. I chewed. I swallowed. I said, "I guess I don't know what you mean."

She pulled the blanket tighter around her shoulders. Her eye makeup was smeared and she looked exhausted. I wasn't used to her coming across so vulnerable. She said, "Do you ever feel like you have this idea of who you want to be? And you try and try and try to be that person, but sometimes you step back and realize it's only pretending. Deep down, no matter what, you're always just you."

I nodded so she'd keep talking, but I couldn't really relate. I'd never pretended to be anything but myself. Not that I'm super fantastic or anything—believe me, I realize that people find my personality abrasive. But it's *me*. It's not like I can open a closet and pick out a new personality the same way I'd pick out a different pair of shoes.

Maylee said, "I fucked up tonight. With the gun."

I said, "Yeah, you did."

Even though I was just agreeing with her, for a second she was defiant. She gazed at me head-on, a fierce look in her eyes, and said, "You did, too, by even bringing it."

I said, "No kidding."

She nodded, pacified. She unwrapped another Tootsie Roll. Then she was like, "Some of the things John said to me in the tent... God, they were so mean. But they were also true. I'm not a good person, Petra. I'm reckless and self-centered and immature."

Look, I love Maylee, but I wasn't going to sit there and tell her that wasn't true, because we'd both know it was a lie.

She said, "You know what John did after saying all that stuff to me? He rolled over and went to sleep. How do you tear into another person and then *sleep*? But I knew he was right. And I kept thinking about the way you all looked at me after I fired the gun. It's like you loathed me. Like all of you loathed me."

I started to speak, but she held her hand up.

The fire sputtered.

Outside, an owl hooted.

Maylee said, "I started to imagine how it would be in the morning. We'd get up and you'd make your sludgy campfire coffee and everyone would be groggy and hungover. For a little bit, I'd think everything was fine and we could pretend last night never happened. But then one of you would look at me, *really* look at me, and I'd see that hatred all over again. I couldn't bear the thought of everyone looking at me that way. I couldn't bear how it would force me to look at myself. So I ran."

I thought that when I heard Maylee's excuse, I'd be even more angry. Instead, I sympathized. I *did* know what she was going through. I knew it just from a few hours ago when Nolan was yelling at me. Sometimes being honest with yourself hurts so much.

I said, "I get it."

Maylee looked surprised. She said, "You do?"

I nodded. And she jumped off the bed and hugged me tight.

[pause]

That's the last time she'll ever hug me.

Oh God.

[crying]

I'm sorry, can you give me a second?

[long pause]

Okay. Sorry. I just—

[pause]

No, that's okay. I'd rather get this over with.

As I was saying, Maylee hugged me. Then she asked if I'd mind if she stayed there overnight.

I told her, "You know the night is practically over?"

She laughed and was like, "You know what I mean."

I did know. She needed to be by herself. Sometimes being alone in nature is the only way to fix your head. So I said yeah. I told her I'd leave her there for the night.

She thanked me. She seemed so appreciative.

I moved to leave, but when I did, I bumped the table. That little purple vase got knocked over, rolled right off the edge. I caught it before it smashed on the floor. Just barely. It was upside down, and I saw black ink on the bottom, spelling out someone's name. You know, the way elementary school teachers label their students' art projects so they don't get mixed up.

Without even thinking about it, I brought the vase closer so I could get a better look.

You know what name was written there?

I bet you can guess, can't you? At this point you probably know more than I do.

It was *A. Buckley*.

43

Abigail, why didn't tell us your
father owns the cabin?

ABIGAIL

        [long pause]

Oh.

        [pause]

I...

        [pause]

I *wanted* to, it's just... I don't know. I was too ashamed, I guess. Because then I'd have to admit I'd been lying all weekend, which I already feel super awful about.

    A few nights ago, Maylee and I were talking about all of this, and she said, "You won't be *lying*, Abigail, just keeping some things to yourself. Don't you do that anyway? Surely you don't tell *everyone* everything." It made sense at the time. Maylee could make pretty much anything seem logical. But once we were actually on the camping trip, I started thinking she was wrong. It felt a whole lot like I was lying.

[pause]

The worst was when I told Nolan I was going to help look for Maylee. Up until then I'd only—what's it called? Lied by omission? But when I left him at the campsite, I *outright* lied.

It's just, while I was sitting by the campfire, I started worrying that Petra and John would check the cabin. Maylee hadn't accounted for that because they weren't even supposed to know about the place. They *wouldn't* have if Nolan hadn't accidentally led us right to it earlier.

I started to get panicky, thinking about Maylee in the cabin alone, not knowing she was about to get caught. I had to warn her. If I could slip past Petra and John and get there first, then...I don't know. I'd tell her what was going on, and she'd come up with a new plan.

So I lied to Nolan and told him I wanted to join the search.

He believed me so easily. He said sure, I should go, and that made me feel a million times worse. He trusted me, and I was letting him down.

[pause]

Nana Abbie always says that when you deceive others, you destroy yourself.

44

Did you ask Maylee about the vase?

PETRA

At first I couldn't even process what I was seeing. I stared at the vase for a long time because I knew it *should* make sense, but it didn't. A. Buckley? *Abigail?*

Eventually I said... God, I feel like such an idiot now, but I said to Maylee, "Did Abigail make this?"

It occurred to me that the vase didn't look *similar* to something I'd made when I was little. Abigail and I were in the same class, I'd taken home some ugly clay creation, too.

I was like, "Why is an art project of Abigail's in this cabin?"

There was a moment where something flashed across Maylee's face. It wasn't shame or anything like that. It was pity. She felt bad about the depths of my cluelessness.

That's when things started falling into place. Abigail's vase was in the cabin because the cabin belonged to her family. And like, okay, even in my confusion, I understood that wasn't exactly a coincidence.

I set the vase back on the table. My hand was shaking. I looked at Maylee and said, "Every single word out of your mouth has been a lie."

45

What exactly was Maylee's plan?

ABIGAIL

> [pause]

I'll tell you everything, because I guess I have to. I just... Well, I told Maylee I wouldn't ever talk about this with anyone. She made me promise; she said, "Abigail, if we're going to do this, it needs to be a secret forever. Even like fifty years from now."

It feels wrong to break a promise to Maylee, even if she's dead. Maybe *especially* since she's dead. That's why I didn't tell you this part right away. And knowing the whole truth couldn't help you save her, so I guess I hoped it'd be okay to keep it secret.

> [pause]

Actually...

> [pause]

I'm still not being honest. I didn't *only* hide this part of the story for Maylee. I did it for myself, too. You know how sometimes when you say something out loud, it makes you realize just how bad it is?

But Nana Abbie says we have to face our wrongs to be right with ourselves, so here's the truth: what Maylee and I did...it was awful.

PETRA

I stared at Maylee, totally in shock.

She tilted her head and looked at me curiously. She said, "You're not going to freak out, are you?"

I couldn't believe how calm she sounded. I told her, "I don't know. Are you going to give me some answers?"

Look, I realize I can be oblivious about some things, okay? I know about the forest, not people. People are mysterious—like Nolan's online friends, for instance. I always say that's not *real* friendship, but the truth is, I just can't fathom connecting with anyone online when I can hardly do it in person.

I also know that I have a blind spot for Maylee. God, you think I don't get that? My dad reminds me of it constantly. Tells me Maylee is trouble—and that she's the sort of person who never gets into trouble alone.

But when you have all the years of friendship that Maylee

and I have between us, you *do* get to know someone in a different way. I knew that deep down there was goodness inside her. So yeah, maybe sometimes I was too forgiving and maybe I overlooked her flaws, but only because she's always done me the same favor of overlooking mine.

Anyway, even with all of that, I wasn't completely freaking naive.

I told Maylee I wanted some answers, but I obviously realized she wasn't going to give me answers I *liked*.

ABIGAIL

When Maylee and I broke up, right at the start of junior year, she said all these things about how we'd still be friends. Except, we just...weren't. I tried texting and calling sometimes, but she never responded. And then she started dating John. I can take a hint, you know? I stopped trying to get in touch with her because I figured that "wanting to be friends" is just something you say in the moment to make a breakup hurt less.

So we hadn't talked for almost a year. And then a few weeks after school started, Maylee came up to me in the cafeteria. I was sitting with some people from choir—

[pause]

Yes, I'm in choir. I have friends.

Gosh, I haven't spent high school sitting around pining for Maylee. I guess it could seem that way since she's the only thing I've talked about for hours. But that's only because she's the reason I'm *here*. I have a whole other life. I go hunting with my dad and do choir and go to movies with my friends. I'm more than just Maylee.

[pause]

Yeah, I know I said it would be nice to make friends with everyone else on the camping trip. But I didn't mean to imply I don't have *other* friends. Nana Abbie always says there's no such thing as too many friends or plants.

Anyhow. I was eating lunch when Maylee came up and said, "I would *kill* for a Frappuccino right now."

After all the months we hadn't spoken, that's how she started a conversation with me. When I replied, I meant for it to sound really firm, you know? But it didn't come out that way. I said, "Nothing is stopping you from getting one."

Besides the fact that it was during school hours and lunch is closed campus. But details like that would never stop Maylee.

She smiled at me. I could feel the whole lunch table watching, my friends wondering what this was about. Maylee pouted and said, "You're not really going to make me go alone, are you?"

[pause]

Just think how different everything would be right now if I wouldn't have gone with her. Maylee might be *alive* still. But I said, and I thought I was being super bold, I said, "Are you buying?"

She laughed and was like, "I'd forgotten how much I like you, Abigail."

Which kinda stung.

I hadn't forgotten how much I liked her.

PETRA

Maylee was still sitting on the cot casually chewing her Tootsie Rolls, but her shoulders had tensed. There was a new alertness in her eyes.

I set the vase down very carefully. It was an effort, because I wanted to smash it to the freaking ground. But it wasn't mine to smash.

I said, "You probably think you can tell me anything and I'll believe it, huh?"

She seemed to really consider it, which made me angrier. Finally she said, "It's not just you. Most people want to believe whatever's easiest."

I said, "I think most people want to be told the truth."

Her response was fast. She said, "I'm not even sure there's such a thing as truth. Not the way you're thinking of it."

Obviously, I told Maylee that I didn't know what the crap she was talking about.

She popped another piece of candy into her mouth and chewed thoughtfully. She said, "Think about it: Right now, at this moment, John's truth is that I'm lost in the woods. Your truth is that I'm here in this cabin. What's true for him isn't what's true for you."

I didn't bother keeping the edge from my voice. I said, "Yes, Maylee, but one of those things is *objectively* true. It's what's *actually happening*. You're in the cabin."

She said, "Or maybe more than one thing can be true at once. Like, maybe we're all living in different realities."

I unclenched my fists. I laid my aching hands flat against the splintery table. I said, "Okay. Sure. Why don't you tell me a little bit about your current reality, then?"

Maylee said, "My current reality? I'm here in the cabin with you. You're furious at me, but you don't even understand what's happening."

I wanted to scream at her. Because that's exactly what I was trying to find out.

ABIGAIL

One day, in the middle of September, Maylee wanted ice cream. We drove to this little shop like forty-five minutes away in the next town over. She said they had the best milkshakes in the world. But I tried the milkshake, and it was...just a shake. I was pretty sure she was still trying not to be seen with me in Wilton.

While we were there, Maylee said, "You know what I was thinking about the other day? The cabin."

I thought about the cabin, too. More than I should, probably.

It was one of the few places Maylee and I could be alone. With, you know...a bed.

[pause]

Oh gosh, I can't believe I'm telling you all of this. It's so embarrassing. But people must admit embarrassing stuff to you all the time, right? Probably this isn't even the worst you've heard. Like, I bet you've had people make terrible confessions to you about, I don't know, murdering their wives or something. So this isn't even anything to be—

Huh?

[pause]

Right. Sorry.

I was saying... What was I saying? Oh, I was saying that Maylee and I couldn't go to either of our houses, so we'd mostly, you know...gosh, okay, we'd mostly fool around in the back seat of Maylee's Beetle. It was super uncomfortable. And one time we were caught by the cops, which was mortifying.

When the police officer knocked on the window, my heart dropped. I started frantically trying to get dressed, and I was so embarrassed that my eyes started to tear up, and I really didn't want to cry. Maylee didn't even flinch, though. She rolled down the window and said, "Hi, Ray. Fancy seeing you here."

I never asked how she knew him. I was just happy he let us go without calling our parents or giving us tickets. Maylee thought the whole thing was hilarious.

After that night, I was super afraid of getting caught again. So I told Maylee that maybe I could sneak my dad's key to the cabin, if she didn't mind the drive. We ended up going there once a week for...I don't know. Months. And it was really great. I know the cabin isn't exactly luxurious, but it's quiet and isolated, and when Maylee and I went there, the rest of the world stopped mattering.

Anyhow, in September, when Maylee asked about the cabin, I nearly dropped my milkshake. We were sitting at a picnic table outside the ice cream shop, and Maylee noticed my reaction; I'm sure she did. But I tried to sound casual and asked, "Why were you thinking about the cabin?"

She said, "I don't know. It was nice there, wasn't it? Lots of good memories."

The best memories.

She said, "Does your dad still have it? He didn't sell it or anything?"

I told her that he still owned it. We still went there every weekend during hunting season.

She said, "Maybe one day we can go there together again."

I didn't know what she meant. Just as friends? Out of nostalgia? Because she wanted to start hooking up again? I wanted to know, but I was afraid to ask. Sometimes it's easier to think that any answer is a possibility.

[pause]

What did *I* want? I don't know. I guess part of me wanted to date her again. But mostly I just wanted to be near her. I just wanted her to stay.

PETRA

I told Maylee, "Maybe this will be easier for you if I ask specific questions."

She snorted and said, "You've never been good at thinking in the abstract, have you?"

Look, I've always been aware of Maylee's flaws, okay? But last night was different. It was like she'd opened herself up and put all her worst parts proudly on display.

I tried to keep my voice even. I said, "The cabin belongs to Abigail."

Maylee said, "If we're being technical, which I'm sure you'd prefer, it belongs to Abigail's dad."

I said, "Okay. And you knew about it before we came to Salvation Creek."

Maylee nodded.

I went on. "This was all some plan, is that right? Abigail knows about this?"

Maylee licked her lips. For a second, her cavalier attitude faltered. She was worried. And that drove a deep spike of fear into my own heart.

She said, "Yes. Abigail knows."

Even though I already knew, hearing Maylee admit it made me angry. I thought about us walking through the forest earlier and Abigail saying we should turn back. I thought about us at the campfire discussing what had happened to Maylee and Abigail nodding along like she was *so* concerned.

They tricked me.

The whole freaking day had been one big trick.

I asked Maylee, "Why? Why would you do this?"

She said, "If I tell you, you'll hate me."

The thing is, I was starting to hate her already.

ABIGAIL

Sometime, I guess toward the end of September, Maylee started talking about being an influencer a lot. Like, all the time. About how much it meant to her, about how it was the only job she could imagine herself doing. She was so passionate about it, the kind of passionate that makes you wonder why you don't care about anything that much.

One day she called me, and she sounded really weird, like she'd been crying. She asked if we could go somewhere. I said yes, of course.

For the longest time she just drove us around town. I'd asked what was going on when I first got into the car, but she wasn't ready to tell me. Maylee never talked about something until she felt really, truly ready. When she finally pulled over, it was into a parking lot. The same one we used to fool around in. I wasn't sure if she realized that or if it was a coincidence. It was dark and felt creepy, which was weird, because it had never seemed that way to me before.

Finally, Maylee said, "My mom hates me."

It wasn't what I was expecting, and I guess that showed on my face, because Maylee was like, "Don't look so surprised. You know how awful she's always been to me."

Did I? Had Maylee mentioned anything like that before? She hardly talked about her family. I pretty much didn't know anything about them other than the fact that her dad wasn't in the picture and that she had a younger sister.

But she must have made comments before about her mom being awful, right? The more I thought about it, the more I had a hazy memory of Maylee saying something like that last year. Still, I said, "I'm sure she doesn't hate you."

Maylee snorted. She said, "You can't possibly understand. People whose parents love them can't even comprehend a parent who *doesn't* love their kid."

I didn't argue because maybe she was right. You probably have certain opinions about my dad—for all I know, you've arrested him before. I definitely realize that he's not even close to perfect. But he never made me feel anything other than loved.

So instead of trying to convince Maylee that she was wrong, because what did I know about it, I asked, "Why does your mom hate you?"

She brushed away a tear and said, "Because she doesn't understand me. She wants me to be like her. Like, go to college and work some soulless job that I hate, because in her mind that's how you become an adult. She can't even recognize that there are other options."

I said, "Like being an influencer?"

Maylee nodded. "We got into another fight about it tonight.

She told me I'm wasting my time. She said... She asked me what makes me so special that strangers would care what I have to say."

My heart broke a little for her. Imagine being told your biggest dreams are worthless. I reached over and put my hand on top of hers. We were quiet for a second, then she said, "More than anything, I want to prove to her that I can do this."

I said, "You will. I believe you will."

She said, "But *how*? I basically have no way to get any further. Like, I'm not going to get famous if I keep posting photos in the same outdated outfits. I need to go to an *actual* salon, not that cheap-ass butcher shop where my mom insists I get my hair cut. I need to travel to interesting locations—no one wants to see pictures of the suburban hell I live in."

I was like, "I never knew being an influencer was so expensive."

She said, "That's not even half of it. I asked my mom to front me some cash, but of course she said no. She literally said she's cutting me off financially if I don't go to college and pick a traditional major. Meanwhile, she's happy to pay for my sister's stupid marching band stuff, like that's any more practical. It's just *me* she hates. She's setting me up to fail."

Maylee started to cry then. Really cry. Dark streaks of mascara ran down her face. And I felt... This is so horrible, I shouldn't even admit it. But I felt grateful that she trusted me enough to open up.

I tried to comfort her, but she was such a mess. She kept saying she needed to leave, she needed to get out of Wilton. She said, "I hate this town. Even the name sucks. I don't want to be chained to some *wilting* town."

Which I thought was kinda sad, because I love Wilton. I could see why it wasn't glamorous enough for Maylee, though.

I told her, "You can leave after high school. You can go anywhere you want."

She said, "But *how*? My mom won't help at all unless I go to college. Do you see, Abigail, even more than the town, it's *her* I need to be free of? She's *controlling* me. All I want is space to be the person I'm supposed to be."

I'm not saying that Maylee's struggle was the hardest struggle. I realize that there are a lot of people facing way worse challenges than she was. But still, she was hurting. I wanted to help. I said, "I saw that Stop and Shop is hiring. Maybe if you got a job there, you could start saving up and—"

She interrupted me and was like, "I *can't* get a regular job. The only way to succeed at anything is by committing yourself, and that means I have to work at being an influencer full time."

I wasn't sure I agreed. Like...aren't there stories about people struggling for years before they make it? But I didn't say that to

Maylee. What did I know? I just listened to her cry and wished there was a way I could help.

PETRA

I asked Maylee, "Were you trying to scare us?"

She frowned and said, "What do you mean?"

I said, "You disappearing and hiding in the cabin—it's some kind of prank, right? You must be trying to freak us out."

She seemed surprised. And then she laughed. Actually *laughed*. She said, "Not everything is about you, Petra."

My head almost exploded. I said, "If you aren't doing it for me, then who?"

She looked at me for a long moment, then said, "Everyone. The whole rest of the world."

ABIGAIL

After the night Maylee broke down, she started bringing up my dad's cabin a lot. She said it would be really nice to go into the woods and clear her head, which I totally understood. But it was hunting season, and my dad was using the cabin every weekend. Finally, Maylee convinced me to ditch the second half of school one Monday.

She drove to Salvation Creek. We rolled all the windows down so the wind whipped through our hair, and she turned the radio up loud and sang along. At one point she said, "God, this is great. I can never convince Petra or John to ditch with me."

I asked why not. She said, "John's too obsessed with his grades to miss class, and Petra is too obsessed with the rules to break them."

It made me feel special in a way. Like Maylee could experience something with me that she couldn't with other people. But at the same time, I wondered if maybe I was making a mistake. Petra and John always seemed smart, so if I was doing something they wouldn't, maybe I should ask myself why.

But then Maylee smiled at me, and I forgot my worries. She reached into the cupholder where she'd stuffed tons of Tootsie Rolls and opened one, swerving on the road as she did.

I'd forgotten that Maylee wasn't a very good driver. She always thought other cars would move for her, the same way kids at school would when she walked the halls. But I guess most of the time she was right.

At the cabin, Maylee plopped down on the cot like it was her own bed. I wasn't sure what to do. A long time ago, I would've stretched out next to her. But that day I sat in one of the chairs at the table. I spun the vase around in a circle—I'd made it in third grade and it was a mess, but my dad says it's one of his prize possessions.

We sat in silence for a little while, but it wasn't comfortable silence. I tried to think of what to say. That's one bad thing about Maylee: it was hard to relax around her. I always felt like I had to find ways to keep her entertained.

Right when I was about to ask if she had a dress for the homecoming dance, Maylee said, "You remember when that girl disappeared last May—the one who got lost and died of exposure?"

Of course I remembered. It happened pretty close to the cabin. My dad had even joined the search party. He said it was awful because he wanted to do his part to help, but he also didn't want to be the one who found her body.

Maylee asked, "Does it scare you to think of someone dying near here?"

I told her it didn't, not really. Jenna Creighton's death was sad, and, gosh, my heart broke for her family. But it didn't *scare* me. I asked Maylee if it scared her.

She said, "Kinda."

She was silent for a moment after that, like she was in deep thought. Then she sat up and grabbed the pillow from the top of the cot and put it on her lap, rested her elbows on it.

The pillow was mine. When I go to the cabin with my dad, he sleeps in a sleeping bag on the floor and gives me the bed. It was weird to have Maylee sitting where I'd slept so many times. Where we used to sometimes take naps together.

Maylee said, "I donated to that fundraiser Jenna Creighton's family set up."

I told her that I had, too.

She said, "You ever think about what happened to all that money after her body was found?"

I hadn't, not even once. I said, "I guess they probably used it to pay for the funeral." My dad says that funerals are just as expensive as weddings—and that both of them celebrate the end of life.

Maylee nodded and seemed to think some more. She said, "What do you think they would have done with the money if Jenna had been found alive?"

I shrugged and said, "I don't know. Maybe hospital bills if she was hurt."

Maylee was like, "You don't think her family would've had to give it back?"

I didn't know—how would I know something like that?—but that I thought it probably didn't work that way.

She said, "You donated. Would you have wanted *your* money back?"

I didn't even have to think about it. Of course I wouldn't. Even if Jenna was found alive, she would have experienced something traumatic, being lost in the woods like that. The last thing I'd do is ask for my five dollars back.

Maylee had this look on her face like I was confirming something she already knew. She said, "I bet most people are the same. No one would have the balls to ask. And people probably donated such small amounts that it wouldn't be worth it anyway."

I nodded, but I was starting to get uncomfortable. The conversation didn't seem casual anymore. It felt like Maylee was leading me down a certain path, and I wasn't sure if I liked it.

So I tried changing the subject. I asked Maylee about some of the pictures she'd posted recently. But she got up and sat down at the table across from me. She said, "Abigail, what if I disappeared?"

PETRA

I crossed my arms over my chest and said, "Okay. You're trying to trick the whole world. Care to explain *why*?"

Maylee sighed and was all, "Petra, I've always known I needed more than this."

When I asked more than *what*, she said, "You know. Wilton. High school. Normal life."

I was like, ooooh-kay. But what else did she think was out there, exactly?

[pause]

The truth is, I *do* think Maylee is special. There's something—

[pause]

I'm doing it again. Present tense. God.

I was going to say there was something dynamic about Maylee. When she walked into a room, people wondered if she was someone important. They went out of their way to talk to her and entertain her and make her happy. I always thought the reason Maylee liked me so much was because I *didn't* try. I was the only one who treated her like a human.

But I didn't know what that had to do with what was happening during our camping trip.

Maylee said, "Seriously, Petra, you need to think bigger. I wasn't planning to come back in the morning. I was going to vanish for like a week. Maybe two."

I stared at her for a long time because it was hard for me to make sense of anything. I said, "You...what? You wanted to stage a disappearance?"

She nodded.

I was like, "But if you didn't come back to the campsite in the morning, I would've called the police. There would've been search parties." I thought about how blond and pretty Maylee was and imagined her smile shining from TVs across the country. I said, "It would have been all over the news."

Maylee beamed at me and shoved another Tootsie Roll into her mouth. She said, "Now you're getting it."

ABIGAIL

Maylee said, "Abigail, what if I disappeared?"

I told her that if she disappeared, I'd be very sad and very worried.

She shook her head and said, "No. I mean what if I disappeared on *purpose*?"

I was starting to understand what she was getting at, but I didn't really want to. So I asked why she'd possibly want that.

She leaned forward and looked at me intently with her golden-brown eyes. And that's when she gave me the whole speech. About how she was dying, literally dying, in Wilton. About how she needed to make it as an influencer to save herself. How only money would let her do that, but she didn't have any way to get money.

She meant any *easy* way, though. I knew it even as I was listening to her. She could have gotten a job. There are ways to make money without faking a disappearance.

Maylee told me it was her only chance. She would disappear. Her sister would set up a fundraiser. She'd be "lost" in the woods for a few days. Maybe even a week. After that, she'd emerge, dirty and scratched up and scared and scarred. And no one would ask for the fundraiser money back, of course. No one would dare.

It was so outlandish that I was having trouble grasping it. I said, "You want to fake your own disappearance?"

She said, "I want *us* to do it."

I was like, "But how would that even work? Where would you *go* for a week?"

Maylee glanced around.

It was like a punch to the stomach. That was why Maylee started talking to me again. That was why she wanted to drive out to the cabin.

Maylee said, "I don't actually need the key; I just need you to unlock it for me. And draw a map of how to get here from a nearby campsite. Oh, and maybe drop some hints to the search party that'll get them looking in the opposite direction."

I didn't say anything. I couldn't even talk. It's like my mind suddenly only had room for one thing, and that was the realization that Maylee had been using me from the start.

It hurt.

It hurt a lot.

Maylee must have guessed what I was feeling, because she reached across the table and grabbed my hand. I wanted to pull away but didn't. She said, "I had to come to you. Not only because of the cabin—the cabin is really just a bonus. I had to come to you because I'm too scared to do this alone, and you're the only one who can help."

I asked why me.

She said, "Because you know the real me. The me I don't let anyone else see. And the situation with my mom—the abuse. You're the only one who knows about that."

She hadn't called it abuse before. But she was right, wasn't she? There are all sorts of ways to abuse someone, and they're not all physical. Her mom was cruel. What *would* it do to Maylee to spend more time in that environment?

She said, "Abigail, getting out of here, doing this, it'll save my life."

I wasn't sure if she meant literally, you know? But I was raised to believe that you always do everything you can to help people. What if doing this really was the only way to save Maylee? On the other hand, how much would it hurt everyone she stole from?

Maylee said, "It's not really stealing if people give the money willingly. Besides, no one will donate *that* much. It'll be a few bucks here and there. People might spend the same amount on a soda. They might lose that much change in their couch cushions. No one is going to suffer from this."

A few dollars here and there to get Maylee out of a really awful situation. That was all.

She said, "If anyone asks for it, I'll give them their money back."

I thought about it for a moment. I said, "I don't get it, though, not exactly. Can't you just use the money to start over somewhere? Do you have to use it to be an influencer?"

She said, "Abigail, what else am I going to do? What other skills do I have? I'm not smart like you. This is my only career path."

I thought she was probably wrong, but she'd been told to give up her dream enough times. The last thing I'd ever do was echo those words.

She squeezed my hand. She said, "Will you do it, Abigail? Will you help me?"

PETRA

I thought about the news coverage, about thoughts and prayers plastered all over social media, about the pictures of Maylee that would hang in every storefront in Wilton. Why would she *want* that?

Except I suddenly had a pretty good guess.

I said, "This is all about your influencer crap, isn't it?"

She was like, "You've said it yourself: I need a niche. You were right. You're always right. It's one of the most annoying things about you."

I wasn't that angry yet. I mean, I was angry. But not *furious*. I was still trying to process everything. Maylee had always been reckless. She'd always been a fan of plots and pranks and schemes. But never anything like this.

She said, "I know I'm pretty, and I know I take good pictures. But what does that matter? With filters today *anyone* can have pretty photos. Beauty isn't a commodity anymore."

I've only been speechless like five times in my life. But that was one of them.

She kept going. "What's my *brand*, Petra? I don't bake or do makeup tutorials or adopt ugly kittens. I'm totally normal. I don't even have good photography equipment. It's exactly like you always told me. I need something to set me apart."

I swallowed. I tried to look at Maylee the same way I'd looked at her that morning. The same way I'd looked at her just a few hours ago. But she wasn't the same person. I said, "So your brand is going to be..."

She said, "The girl who came back from the dead, obviously."

Obviously.

Maylee pulled her blanket tighter around her shoulders. Her eyes were dancing. Why wasn't she remorseful or embarrassed or ashamed? She said, "Imagine it. I disappear in the forest long enough for people to start planning my memorial service. Then I come back."

I said, "I'm sure you'd perfectly cultivate your look. Lost-in-the-forest chic."

She said, "Exactly."

She'd *need* the perfect look, of course, because the world would be watching. There'd be photos and news clips of someone—some search and rescue person, some detective—helping poor Maylee into the back of an ambulance. She'd emerge from the forest looking fragile but triumphant. I could picture it all too well.

I said, "And then what?"

She said, "And then I'll leverage that into a career. I'm sure I'll get new followers from disappearing alone. I mean, do you realize that Jenna Creighton's follower count is *still* going up daily?"

I said, "No, Maylee. I didn't realize that. Because I don't stalk dead people's social media."

She snorted. I couldn't believe that she was able to laugh. She said, "Then I'll launch this whole campaign. I almost died, so naturally I'd want to have as many new experiences as possible. Sort of like one hundred things to do before you die. Only the opposite. I'll be getting a second chance at life."

I hated that she was right. It was a good hook.

The girl who disappeared; the girl who came back.

Maylee said, "I'll even make sure to visit all these national parks. Can you imagine? People will talk about how *brave* I am.

Willingly facing the wilderness again after I had such an ordeal there. I bet I'll get sponsorships from camping brands."

She'd thought of everything. She must have been planning this for a long time. I couldn't believe it...but I also *could*.

Maylee went on, talking about how she might even get a book deal, tell the harrowing story of what she went through when she was lost in the woods. She stopped, thinking, then said, "I'll need content for that, like forest survival stuff. I bet you could help brainstorm some ideas."

I was like, "Oh my God, Maylee, I'm not *helping* you."

She shrugged and said, "Fine, I can do it on my own. I just figured you'd make it more authentic."

She was serious. She'd truly thought I'd help her. And that made me think...when you're with a person who assumes they can convince you to do anything, was Maylee the problem, or was *I*? How many times over the years had I given in to her? How many times had I gone along with a scheme against my better judgment? And when you keep taking steps back, even if they're small at first, one day do you suddenly realize all those small steps have turned into miles?

I was silent for a moment. I rotated the purple vase a half turn. I said, "I guess you roped Abigail into all of this because you needed the cabin."

Maylee shrugged.

I said, "And Abigail is okay with this plan? She wants to help you become the world's most famous victim?"

Maylee grinned—she actually *grinned*—and she said, "What a title. The world's most famous victim. Honestly, I don't hate it. But anyway, yeah. Abigail gets how important this is to me."

And she just went along with it, no questions asked? I didn't buy it. My head was spinning, and I felt like crying. I told Maylee, "I have no idea which parts of this are true."

Maylee said, "It's all true. You're the only person I've *ever* been able to tell the whole truth to. You're the only one who understands me."

I was squeezing my hands into fists again. I could feel my nails cutting into my palms. I said, "Funny that you didn't want me involved in the first place, then."

ABIGAIL

I didn't agree to Maylee's scheme right away.

I thought about it for a week.

Every night I lay in bed, the window open to let in the autumn air. I listened to the sounds of Sunny Acres: A dog barking. Kids playing basketball. Mr. Wade next door working on the same truck he'd been working on for years—I'd started to realize the whole point was to work on it, not actually get it running.

I thought and thought, and I kept imagining Maylee at her

own house, in her own bed. Had she just sat through another dinner where her mom berated her? Had she been made to feel small and worthless? Had she cried herself to sleep?

Lying about Maylee disappearing felt slimy. But if you do something bad with good intentions, does that make it good or bad?

I finally decided to talk to my dad about it. Kinda. I didn't tell him the details because he definitely wouldn't have approved. But I found him one night sitting at the table in our tiny laminate-covered kitchen. I pulled a chair out from the table and it screeched across the floor. My dad got the chairs cheap when the Dixie Pig went out of business. Do you remember that? They auctioned off all their stuff. Sometimes it's pretty weird to think that when I sit at my kitchen table, I'm sitting where a hundred strangers' butts have been before. It's like—

[pause]

Right, sorry.

Anyhow, that night I said, "Dad, can I talk to you about something?"

He was doing a sudoku puzzle from the big book I got him for Christmas. People think my dad isn't smart, and I guess he's not. He doesn't know big words, and he hasn't read many books. But you should see the way he does sudoku.

My dad turned off the hunting podcast he was listening to and said, "What's happening, baby girl?"

I thought for a moment and said, "Can something be both bad and good at the same time?"

He said, "Well, sure. Ain't nothing in the world that's only one thing."

"But like...what if there was something you did? Like a deliberate action. And it hurt a lot of people in a little way, but it helped one person in a big way?"

My dad put down his pen and said, "You getting yourself caught up in something, Ab?"

I told him no.

He looked at me for a long, long time and was like, "I trust you, so I won't ask more about that." Then he said, "I always felt there were some rules for following and some rules for breaking, and what's important is having the brains to know the difference."

But that was the problem. What if I didn't have the brains?

My dad tapped his pen against the table. The kitchen clock ticked. Outside, I heard the sound of someone firing a pistol in the back alley. Finally, he said, "You remember the time we seen a deer after the season ended? Shooting was illegal, but that year was real lean for us. So I killed it. I knew it was wrong, but did it anyhow, because it'd stock our freezer full and put food in my kid's belly. What do you say: Was it wrong or not?"

He never gave me a concrete answer, but I felt like I understood what he was getting at.

So I thought some more. And some more.

Eventually, I called Maylee and said, "Okay. I'll do it."

She said, "Awesome."

And I could tell from her voice that she knew I'd agree to it all along.

Then I said, "But it has to be this weekend."

That sure got her attention. She said, "You're talking five days from now?"

I said yes, it was the only way she could hide out in the cabin. My dad was staying there every weekend. Except the coming weekend, *this* weekend, he had to skip it. A friend of his hooked him up with a weeklong job in Boise installing drywall. His contracts had been slow coming lately, and the Boise job was good money. This weekend would be the only one in fall he wasn't using the cabin.

Maylee said, "This isn't exactly what I was expecting. But...I've always liked improvising. Five days, then."

Five days and Maylee would disappear.

Then she said, "I'll call you back in a little bit. I need to get ahold of Petra and convince her to do the camping trip."

And I was wondering, *what* camping trip?

46

John, at that point, you were unaware
that Maylee was at the cabin, correct?

JOHN

Maylee *was* there? You're telling me Petra was right?

But then how...

[pause]

I'm sorry, I'm confused.

Does this have anything to do with the person I heard
walking through the woods?

[pause]

I already told you, *yes*, I'm positive it was a person.

Deer don't carry flashlights.

I didn't get a good look at them, though. When I heard
footsteps and saw the light, I ducked behind a tree and hid.

[pause]

Was it Maylee's killer that I heard? Was she at the shack because... Was she being held captive?

47

Nolan, based on your previous statements,
it's clear you left the campsite. Why?

NOLAN

I'm not big on wandering the woods alone in the middle of the
fucking night—but guess what I'm also not cool with? Sitting
around like a *sacrifice*.

The longer I'm alone, the more my paranoid animal brain
starts to take over.

Bigfoots are intelligent, you know? I'm not saying they have
human levels of reasoning, but they're not bears or deer, either.
If one has been watching us all day, then it knows its best chance
is to get us separate. And me being alone at the campsite, I'm the
easiest to pick off.

Plus, I'm stressing about Petra running into the creature
in the forest. Knowing her, she'd be so pissed a bigfoot was

interfering with her carefully coordinated schedule that she'd try to fight it. Something like that happens, Petra won't even realize how much danger she's in.

I already screwed up bad, freezing while the bigfoot took Maylee. In that moment, I was every awful thing she'd said about me. Useless. Pathetic. A coward. The kind of person who'd wait to die instead of taking action.

I don't want to be that person, though.

And I don't have to be.

Right now, this moment, I can change.

So I decide to go into the woods—to save Petra and to save myself. I take a flashlight and my thermal imager, not because I'm still trying to gather data, but because I think it might help locate the others. Believe me, by that point, all my plans to document the bigfoot are shot. I'd been wrong to try in the first place. I hadn't known what I was getting into.

My goal is to find Petra and John and Abigail and convince them there's nothing we can do for Maylee. I'll drag them back to the campsite, get them into the car. We won't even pack our stuff, we'll just *go*. As soon as we're on the main highway, we can call the police.

Let *them* find Maylee.

Let them come in with tracking dogs and helicopters and enough noise and people that it'll scare the bigfoot off.

All I need to do is find everyone and convince them this is the best strategy.

That's it.

So I leave the campsite. I walk down the hill, toward the creek.

48

What happened next, Petra?

PETRA

You probably think I was massively underreacting, don't you? You're probably wondering how I could have sat there listening to Maylee talk about her grand plan and stayed semi calm.

It's like this: You know how sometimes you'll get hurt—like maybe you'll burn yourself while cooking—but even though you watch it happen, it takes a second before you can *feel* it? I heard what Maylee was saying, but my brain couldn't fully process it.

I stood in the cabin and tried to make sense of everything. I thought about how when Maylee disappeared, people would be terrified. Her mom, her sister, John. Me. What about *me*? When days passed and there was no sign of her, I would've gotten more and more scared. I've been involved with search and rescues. I know when it looks like someone isn't coming back.

And Maylee didn't care. She didn't care about the tears we'd cry. About the nights of sleep we'd lose. About the absolute despair we'd feel knowing she was lost in the woods. She didn't care that we'd be wondering where she was sleeping that night or if she'd found food and water.

Not to mention the bigger implications. How many people would give up their time for a pointless search effort? How much money would be wasted? When the police department was focusing its efforts on finding Maylee, how many other crimes could they have been solving?

Maylee had big dreams, but she'd never been willing to work for them. She saw an easy way to become famous and jumped at the chance. She was completely incapable of seeing what massive harm she was doing.

At that point my numbness wore off, and my mind basically went red with rage. I stood up and said, "You're the most selfish person I've ever met."

Maylee thought about it for a second and calmly said, "I'm sure that's not true."

But it was—it *was*.

I said, "I can't believe you think I'd go along with this scheme. I can't believe you'd have the nerve to even tell me about it. This is the most disgusting thing I've heard in my life."

Annoyance flashed in her eyes. She said, "Get a grip, Petra."

I was like, "Get a grip? Get a freaking grip? You're committing a crime and ruining lives, and you want me to *get a grip*?"

Maylee stood up, too, the flannel blanket falling from her shoulders. This blows my mind, but *she* was actually mad at *me*. She said, "The only reason you even care is because I'm doing something you can't control, you fucking obsessive freak."

I almost hit her. I've never hit anyone in my life, but right then I wanted to.

I didn't though, okay? Just in case there are... Just in case you see marks on the body, it wasn't me. I didn't touch her.

And I didn't kill her. I was enraged, but I never would have...

[pause]

Sorry. Anyway.

I told Maylee, "No, I care because this is illegal and dangerous and harmful and...just evil, Maylee. How do you not see that?"

She said, "You have it easy, Petra. You have it so easy that you can't even comprehend that some people don't. You have your nice little blended family, parents who love you. You have it *all*. So stop judging me. You don't know anything about me."

I said—well, I guess I kind of shouted it: "What are you talking about? I know *everything* about you."

But I already realized that wasn't true at all.

That's when I decided I had to get out of there. I told Maylee I was leaving.

The anger went out of her so fast that it made me dizzy. How could she turn her feelings on and off so easily? In this kind of wheedling voice, she said, "Don't tell John and Nolan, okay? Wait, and let's talk about this tomorrow."

I stared at her in shock. I said, "John and Nolan? Maylee, they're the least of your worries. I'm calling the police."

That was my plan. For the most part. Technically, my plan was to get out of there, find a place with signal, and call my dad. I wasn't sure what he'd do, exactly.

Maylee's eyes went wide. She was like, "You wouldn't."

I said, "You know I will."

Then she turned panicky. She started pleading, saying, "Petra, no. I'll get in so much trouble. Everyone will hate me."

I...I told her, "Then everyone will know how I feel."

I moved toward the door. She grabbed my sleeve, and I shook her off. She grabbed me again, this time just above my elbow, hard enough to hurt. I tried to jerk away, but she didn't let go, and we had this...not a fight, but a scuffle, I guess. At one point she reached up and I think she was trying to grab my hair, but I moved away too fast, and she dragged her nails across my face.

[pause]

Yeah, I know what I told you about the scratches earlier, but I was flustered, okay? Are you really not used to people getting nervous when they talk to you? God.

[pause]

Anyway.

I pulled back from her and she...she came at me again. There was this look of panic and anger on her face. Like she'd never considered she might get caught, and she would do anything—*anything*—to stop me from going to the police.

I hope I'm wrong. I hope that in the moment, with emotions running high, Maylee came off as more aggressive than she actually was. Because right then, the way she looked, I was sure she wanted to hurt me. My *best friend* wanted to hurt me.

I got scared, okay? I needed to get away from her.

Before she could touch me again, I ran.

49

Let's step back for a second. At this
point, to the best of your knowledge,
where was the rest of your group? We're
trying to pinpoint everyone's location
in the moments before Maylee died.

PETRA

How are you unclear on this? Am I supposed to...what? Do your
job for you?

I'd left the cabin and was walking back to the campsite—
Nolan and Abigail were waiting there. I assumed John was still
cowering on the rock across the creek.

I can draw you a map if you want. No, I'm not being sarcastic. I'm asking you seriously, do you want me to draw you a
freaking map?

NOLAN

I'm alone in the woods.

I have no idea where anyone else is. I want to call out for them, but I can't draw attention to myself.

I'd thought Abigail would be right ahead of me, but she's not. I need to find her and the others—my sister, especially—and get out. They could be anywhere, though.

And the bigfoot, it could be anywhere, too.

JOHN

I was sneaking through the woods. It was pitch-black—no moonlight, even—and my flashlight was starting to dim. Petra probably had replacement batteries, but as far as I knew, she was still at the shack. I can't say for sure, though. I'd wandered decently far from where we'd split up.

[pause]

I thought the campsite must be just ahead.

Except I'd been thinking that for a while.

It suddenly occurred to me that maybe I overshot it. Maybe I was heading deeper into the forest, away from civilization.

ABIGAIL

Nolan was still at the campsite. That's where I'd left him, and

I knew he wouldn't venture into the woods alone. But I had no idea where John and Petra were.

I'd stayed off the path I thought they'd taken, but shouldn't I have heard them calling for Maylee? When they first went into the woods, Petra had been shouting Maylee's name constantly. I didn't know why she'd stopped.

Since I was trying to get to Maylee quickly while avoiding the others, I needed to come at the cabin from the other side. I cut through the woods near our campsite, but couldn't find a place to cross the creek, not in the dark. And while I was looking...

This is embarrassing to admit. But I got all turned around. I should have known better. I'd grown up in those woods. I *know* how easy it is to lose your way.

But there was no use thinking about how things should have been. I was already lost.

50

We understand the next part is hard to talk
about. But we're almost done. You can go home
soon. You'd like that, wouldn't you? You
just need to tell us what happened next.

ABIGAIL

Everything is a blur. Being alone in the forest. Nolan running
up to me, shaking and crying. Petra shouting that we had to find
Maylee.

It feels like I'm looking at it through dirty glass. I'm not trying
to hide anything from you, I swear. I'm trying to remember when
exactly everything happened, but it's all jumbled and there's so
much I don't understand.

Like why did Maylee leave the cabin? She was safe there.
She was killed in the woods, but she wasn't even supposed to *be*
in the woods, not right then.

Part of me keeps thinking...I don't know. What if Petra

found her at the cabin and got really angry? What if she... What if she hurt Maylee? If you think about it, wouldn't it be easier for someone to get away with a crime if their parent was in law enforcement?

But that doesn't make sense, either, because the gunshot I heard was close by. And then John walked out of the trees with blood on his hands. So it couldn't have been Petra who killed Maylee because it was John... Wasn't it?

PETRA

I passed the rock where I'd left John, and he wasn't there. Which, as you can probably imagine, was very freaking alarming.

I sat down and tried to think of what to do. I couldn't concentrate, though. I felt sick and scared and exhausted. My stomach twisted, and my eyes burned. Finally, I gave in and cried. I don't know how much time passed. Once I started sobbing, I couldn't make myself stop. It felt like something vital was being ripped out of me. I kept thinking that no matter what happened next, Maylee and I would never go back to the way we were. I couldn't unlearn everything I'd found out about her.

And yeah, it hurt, okay? Maylee might have been a lot of terrible things, but she was also my best friend. Knowing our friendship was over... It almost felt like someone had died. That's what I thought at the time. It seems ridiculous now. When I was crying on the rock, there was still so much possibility. I hadn't understood how truly final something could be.

After a while I started walking again. I needed to find the others. I needed to tell Nolan and John that Maylee was okay, and I needed to tell Abigail that I knew everything. Then I needed to call my dad. I really needed to call my dad.

NOLAN

I already told you this part of the story. I told you right at the beginning.

[pause]

You need me to go through the whole thing again, really?

[pause]

Fine. Okay.

I'm walking through the forest.

I don't know how much time passes. It feels like hours, but I guess it couldn't have been. I'm stumbling around, breathing heavy. I keep tripping because I'm trying to keep an eye on what's ahead of me and on my phone at the same time. The thermal imager is showing blues and greens. Nothing around me is giving off heat.

I pass this tree with a branch so low it almost bashes me

across the face. And then later—a few minutes, an hour, I don't know—I pass the same tree. I've been going in circles. Or have I been? How can I really tell one tree from another? Everything in the forest seems the same.

I trip and fall, landing hard on my ass. Try to stand and get rocked by a wave of vertigo. When it passes, I get to my feet more carefully. I blink a few times because the whole world seems blurry. I reach up and touch my forehead. It stings. A bump? A cut? I can't even tell what's happening to my own body.

The creek is rushing nearby, and I stop and listen to it for a moment.

I hear a snap.

A branch breaking. Right near me.

I slowly, carefully look around.

I point my camera in the direction the sound came from.

Then comes a new noise, a soggy noise, like something heavy and wet slopping onto the ground. It's not the creek splashing over rocks. This sound is nothing like that.

That's when the thermal imager picks up a flash of red. Movement in the trees. Something is there, something is *there*. I'm terrified. I want to run and hide—but it's like there's a voice in my head calling me pitiful, worthless. Telling me that I've come this far, I'd be a coward to leave without making sure what I'm seeing is real.

So I move closer. It's so dark. My flashlight beam isn't doing shit, and I'm mostly relying on the thermal imager. I try to be quiet, but I snap a few twigs. The thing in front of me, the red blur on the thermal imager, stops. Like it's listening.

The forest is too quiet. I know that's a bad sign. Don't ask me why, I don't have any answers, but the woods always get silent when a bigfoot is around.

I move closer still. The shape... It moves. Begins to stand up. That's when I see for the first time that it's a biped. Beyond a doubt. And I'm shocked. Why am I shocked when this is exactly what I was expecting?

I think about whispering Petra's name. Or Abigail's or John's. Because the shape might be one of them, right?

But when the creature reaches its full height, I know that's not possible. It's seven feet tall at least. Maybe taller.

And then my flashlight hits in just the right way, and I get a glimmer of eyeshine. Blue eyeshine. That's what makes me certain. That's when I know beyond a doubt what I'm looking at. What's looking back at me.

The bigfoot stares at me, and I know I'm about to die. Out there in the woods at Salvation Creek, I'm about to get ripped apart. But a second later, I realize no, not *me*. The creature bends down, and I see that it's already at work mauling something else.

Some*one* else.

Maylee.

It carried Maylee away from our campsite. It brought her here. And now it's eating her.

JOHN

I stumbled through the forest. I wasn't sure where I was going, but I knew I had to keep moving. So that's what I did. I moved.

Eventually I heard voices.

ABIGAIL

I was near the creek, all turned around and confused. I wasn't trying to get to Maylee at that point; I just wanted to find my way out of the woods. So I called out to the others. A moment later, Nolan came bursting out of the trees. I was only relieved to see him for like a split second because his face was deathly pale and he was sobbing.

He kept saying something about an animal, and I asked, "What was it? Was it a bear?"

But he shook his head and said that it was... He said it was a bigfoot. I guess I don't want to say that's impossible, because only God knows what's truly possible or not. But I thought he probably hadn't actually seen a bigfoot.

I was about to ask him if he was *positive* it wasn't a bear, but I didn't get a chance, because that's when I heard the gunshot.

I jumped.

I kept thinking, "The gun, the gun."

I had forgotten about it.

Who had taken it earlier?

My first thought wasn't that someone got shot. My mind was racing. I was thinking about the animals in the forest, that Nolan really *had* seen something. And Petra must have the gun—who else would have it?—and if she shot at something, it's because she was being attacked.

But one shot from a pistol wouldn't be enough to kill a bear.

Which meant Petra was in big trouble.

I started to tell Nolan we had to help her.

[pause]

No, I didn't know how I intended to do that. I told you. I wasn't thinking straight. I was scared and tired and cold, and Nolan wouldn't stop babbling about the bigfoot, about how the bigfoot had been eating Maylee. My head was a mess.

And that was when John stepped out of the trees.

He had blood on his hands.

JOHN

I went toward the sound of the voices—it wasn't hard, they

were loud and panicked. I didn't stop to think about what that might mean.

That's how I found Nolan and Abigail. His whole body was shaking. Abigail's hands were on his shoulders. She was telling him to breathe. She was telling him she didn't understand.

He was crying so hard that I couldn't make out any words at first. Then I realized he was saying, "It's eating her."

NOLAN

After I see the creature, I guess I run deeper into the woods. I don't remember. I find Abigail, but I don't know exactly how that happens, either.

Somehow I end up on my knees, and I try to stand up, but my legs are shaking too bad to hold me. I'm having trouble breathing.

I try to tell Abigail what happened. She's responding, but her words have this weird slow-motion quality, and I can't quite catch them.

Then John appears out of nowhere shouting about how we need to run. Abigail looks at him and starts saying... I don't remember exactly. Something like, "What did you do?"

I have no idea what either of them are talking about.

PETRA

I didn't even know what I walked into.

One second I was alone in the woods. The next I'd followed shouting and flashlight beams into a clearing where John and Abigail and Nolan were all losing their freaking minds.

Abigail was shouting at John, and Nolan was bent over crying and hyperventilating, and then John ran over to the creek and vomited.

I tried asking what was going on.

I mean, the four of us hadn't been separated *that* long. What could have possibly happened?

ABIGAIL

At first I thought John was hurt, because his hands were so bloody, and he was obviously scared. He kept saying over and over, "We have to get to the car, we have to get to the car." I thought he meant because that's where the first aid kit was. But he was walking around fine for someone who was wounded and didn't seem to be in pain. That's when I realized the blood must not be his.

My mind was moving so fast: John and Petra went into the woods together. I heard a gunshot. And John showed up *without* Petra and with blood all over him.

He shot her.

He must have *killed* her.

What other possibility was there?

Then Petra stepped out of a thick patch of trees, and I almost fell over because for a second I thought I was seeing a ghost.

Huh?

No, of course I don't normally see ghosts. I was super confused, okay? Everything was happening fast, and there was yelling and crying and panicking, and you can't really understand how chaotic it was.

Petra started demanding that someone tell her what was going on *right now*, and it was like being in a dream, where you never stop to think if something makes sense, and I thought, "Wow, Petra is just as pushy dead as she was alive."

A second later I kinda, I don't know, woke up or something. I realized Petra wasn't a ghost, and John hadn't shot her, because she wasn't even bloody. Then I wondered who *had* been shot. There was only one of us missing.

I asked Nolan, "Are you sure you saw Maylee? Are you *sure*?"

Nolan said yes, yes, he saw her.

Petra was freaking out; I think she might have been crying, actually. And she said, "You saw Maylee? Where? We need to get her."

And Nolan told her it was too late.

He said the bigfoot was already eating her.

John started vomiting.

Petra screamed at Nolan, "Don't you dare make this about Bigfoot—don't you *dare*, Nolan."

I guess around then is when I started tuning Petra and Nolan out because everything had finally clicked into place. It was *Maylee* who'd been shot.

John murdered her.

PETRA

Nolan had the nerve to tell me Bigfoot ate Maylee, and I just... I kinda lost it. His cryptid theories are barely tolerable under normal circumstances, but we were in the middle of a freaking *emergency*.

Abigail grabbed my arm like she was trying to yank it from the socket and told me we needed to get away from John because he shot Maylee. Which, at the time, sounded as absurd as Nolan's Bigfoot talk. Now...I don't know. God, watch Abigail Buckley have been right this entire time.

Anyway, I shook her off and was like, "What are you even talking about?"

She said, "Look at his hands. They're bloody."

But his hands weren't bloody.

I looked, and they weren't.

NOLAN

I keep trying to tell Abigail that John didn't shoot Maylee. I *saw* what killed her. But she won't listen.

ABIGAIL

Finally, Petra screamed at the top of her lungs, "Everyone, *shut up!*"

John immediately said, "Keep your voice down. He'll hear you."

Nolan nodded fast like he agreed. He was still trembling, and kept glancing over his shoulder at the trees he'd come from.

Petra looked at me and said, "Abigail, John did *not* kill Maylee."

I told her that he had blood on him.

John kept shaking his head and opening his mouth like he had things to say but had forgotten how to speak.

Petra said, "Look, Abigail."

She grabbed one of John's hands and shined her flashlight onto it. There was no blood.

How?

I knew what I'd seen.

I knew it.

51

Abigail, earlier you told us you heard the
gunshot before you saw Nolan. Now you're
saying the gunshot happened after you
and Nolan were together. Which is it?

ABIGAIL

I said that?

[pause]

I...

[pause]

I'm not trying to lie to you. I promise I'm not. I just... I don't
remember.

[pause]

No. I do. It *must* have been after Nolan and I were together. I'm almost certain.

[pause]

Are you sure that's not what I said earlier?

52

All right, John. We know you've been
holding back, but we haven't pressed
it. Now it's time to be honest. We need
to know what happened in the woods.

JOHN

[pause]

Can I talk to my lawyer privately?

[long break]

Okay. I'm ready.

To start, I want to say I haven't lied.

Just so we're clear on that. I never lied to you.

But let's be real. You've looked at me like a suspect from the
second we walked into the station—like I was guilty before you
even knew there was a crime. When you separated the four of us,

you pulled me away first. Maylee dying is the worst thing that's ever happened to me, but I haven't been able to start mourning because I'm wondering if I'll be spending the rest of my life locked in a cell.

Under the circumstances, it's been difficult to be forthcoming.

Here it is, though: I knew Maylee was dead before we came here. And I...

[pause]

I don't know how to talk about this.

It hurts so much, and I still—

[breaks off crying]

I'm sorry.

[pause]

Actually, I'm *not* sorry. I deserve a minute to grieve. It's completely unfair the way you—

[long pause]

Okay.

My lawyer advises me to stay calm.

So I'm calm.

And I'll tell you what happened last night.

I think you realize that I've never been into the idea of camping. I'm not used to the woods like Petra or Abigail. I like paved roads. I like eating in restaurants and sleeping in a bed.

I also like making my parents happy, and they *really* weren't cool with the trip. We got into a fight about it. I almost never fight with my mom and dad—they're smart people, right? If they're saying not to do something, there's probably a good reason.

But I pushed back about the camping trip, and we argued. My dad eventually came around to my side. Said he didn't like the idea of me running around the woods, either, but they had to let me live my life. He reminded my mom that next year I'd be away at college and they'd better get used to not knowing exactly where I am or what I'm doing.

[pause]

Why did I fight with my parents when I don't even like camping?

[pause]

I told myself it was for Maylee—because she seemed so excited about camping...and about spending the night together. But the truth is, I went on the trip for *me*. I guess I wanted to step out of my comfort zone. Prove something to myself. I don't know.

I realized my mistake before we even got to the campsite.

It started when we passed that gas station with the *Sasquatch Crossing* sign. You like scary movies? Well, I don't. Maylee loves them, though, so we've watched tons together. And I've seen gas stations like the one at Salvation Creek a million times. If we'd stopped there, some old white dude with missing teeth would've warned that if we went into the woods, we'd never come back again.

Everyone else would have ignored him, just like they ignored the other disturbing shit—I'm sorry, stuff—that piled up once we got to Salvation Creek. The footprint. The shack. The strange noises. We were getting hit with one bad omen after another, and nobody else was entertaining the possibility that someone—not Bigfoot, but a *person*—was out there with us.

And that's why I'm talking to you now. Maybe you'll still try to pin this on me. But I can't sit here and keep what I saw to myself. Because Maylee was... She was murdered last night. Someone shot her straight through the heart and...

[pause]

Give me a second, please.
I'm telling you everything, so please just bear with me.

[blows nose]

I love Maylee, you know?

She could be frustrating sometimes, and yes, we'd just gotten into an argument, but that doesn't mean I loved her any less.

I know some people don't understand it. A bunch of my friends say I shouldn't waste my time with her. They think she plays with people's feelings, that she'll ditch me as soon as she's bored. But they're wrong.

Did I tell you when Maylee and I got together? It was only a few weeks after the car accident. Andy had just come out of the coma, but people were still looking at me like I was a criminal. Maylee wasn't put off by the drama that came with dating me, though. She never judged me. She never judged *anyone*. A lot of people overlook her good qualities, but I always saw them.

Even when Maylee first went missing, I knew in my heart that she wasn't just lost. Maybe she willingly left the tent to go to the bathroom or grab something from the car. But once she was out there alone, in the middle of the night, someone grabbed her. Someone who'd been watching us all day and waiting for the right opportunity.

Searching the woods while knowing there was a predator nearby was one of the most terrifying moments of my life. And when Petra went to the cabin by herself, when I was alone in the dark, listening to someone creep through the woods...

Look, I tried to stay rational, I did. I kept thinking about what Petra would say if she were with me. Kept telling myself my imagination was working overtime. It was that horror movie Maylee and I watched before the trip, right? It had put ideas in my head. There was nothing in the forest with me. Nothing.

Maybe I could've convinced myself if I'd been the only one experiencing anything. But all day Maylee was hearing and seeing weird stuff, too. Even Nolan's Bigfoot evidence proved that someone—another *human*—was at Salvation Creek. It *wasn't* in my head. I could sit there all night and tell myself I was overreacting, but how did that account for Maylee and Nolan?

Then I saw movement from the corner of my eye. Deep in the trees there was the glow from a flashlight. No mistaking it. I wasn't alone. Something in me snapped. I felt exposed. I felt like I was being hunted.

So I ran.

As I moved through the trees, I kept hearing noises nearby—rustling sounds, footsteps snapping twigs. I kept going—not fast enough, though. Running through the woods isn't like running around the school track. Branches hit me in the face; my feet kept getting tangled in vines. I knew I should be quiet, but I was panting so loud the whole forest could probably hear me. I'd dropped my flashlight somewhere—I couldn't remember when I'd last had it—and could barely see.

I stopped suddenly, nearly crashed into a tree.

There was someone ahead of me in the woods.

[pause]

How far?

A few yards, maybe. Far enough that I couldn't make the figure out very well, not in the dark.

Then the person moved, and I saw a flash of blond hair.

It was Maylee. I'd found her. She was standing on a rise, hunched over like she was... I'm not sure, exactly. It looked like she was taking her shoes off, but I can't figure why she'd be doing that. She hadn't heard me come up, and I tried to call to her, but I was gasping for breath and couldn't get sound to come out. So instead, I started moving forward. I was so close, when—

[pause]

Fuck.

I don't want to say this.

[pause]

No, I know I need to. Just...give me a second.

[pause]

All right.

I'd nearly reached Maylee, and she still hadn't noticed me.

That's when I saw something behind her. Another person sneaking through the trees. I froze. It felt like my whole body turned to stone.

And I was standing right there, *right there*, nearly close enough to reach out and grab Maylee, when the other person raised a gun and shot her.

Maylee collapsed.

I shouted.

I fell to my knees next to her and pressed my hands to the bullet wound, tried to stop the bleeding. Her shirt was soaking wet—how had she bled so much so fast? I—

[pause]

Sorry. I'm just... I don't know. Telling it to you feels like reliving it.

I remember the smell of her blood—like rusty metal. I remember being surprised by how cold it was. I remember watching Maylee's chest for the rise and fall of breath, but she wasn't moving. Her hands were so pale. I kept looking at them because I didn't want to look at the wound, and I didn't want to look at her face because—

[pause]

Sorry.

I couldn't look at her eyes. I couldn't bear to see her eyes without any life in them.

A branch snapped nearby, and I jerked back from Maylee. I thought the killer was coming for me. But he wasn't. He was moving *away*, toward the sound of a voice I'd only just noticed. It was Abigail calling out for us. The killer was heading right toward her.

My first thought was... It was relief. If I stayed where I was, maybe I could still get out of the situation alive.

Then Abigail shouted again. "Hello? Can anyone hear me?"

She might as well have shined a spotlight on herself. How could I leave her like that—her or any of the others? They had no idea what they were up against, had no way to protect themselves. If I didn't get to them fast, they'd end up like...like Maylee.

I got to my feet.

I swallowed my fear.

And I left Maylee.

I left her alone in the dirt, for scavengers to—

[pause]

I'm sorry.

I just...

No one deserves to die like that. No one. I'll probably never forgive myself for abandoning her, but what was I supposed to do? There were other people in danger.

Maybe I'm just making excuses.

[pause]

I left Maylee and ran through the forest toward Abigail's voice, swinging away from the route I saw the killer take. I got there ahead of him, burst into a clearing, and there were Abigail and Nolan, *alive*. We didn't have much time. I tried to explain what had happened, that we were all in danger.

Then Petra was suddenly there saying we needed to find Maylee, and Nolan was talking about Bigfoot, and I knew the killer was going to step out of the trees at any moment. We had to *leave*, there was no time, but no one listened. And then Abigail looked at me—right into my eyes—and called me a murderer, which was... I don't know what to say. It ripped me apart.

Everyone's voices were overlapping. It made me dizzy, it was too much at once, and I started to vomit. I heaved until there was nothing left. Then I went to the creek, swished water in my mouth, rinsed my face. The water was so cold that it hurt, but it didn't snap me out of my panic or confusion. I tried to stand up and vomited again.

Maylee's killer still hadn't come out of the forest, and my brain was going to this weird place that was half terrified, half numb, entirely uncomprehending. I tried to tell the others again that the woods weren't safe, but my mouth wasn't forming words right. A buzzing started in my head, and I just...stood there. It's like I left my body and was looking down, wondering which of us would die next.

[pause]

That's my story.

That's what happened to Maylee.

Go ahead and arrest me for her murder if that's what you have to do. But then, while I'm sitting in a cell, I hope you start to doubt yourselves. I hope you decide to keep the case open, look for other suspects, see if there's anything you missed.

Because, believe me, you'll have gotten the wrong guy.

Maylee's killer is still out there.

53

Nolan, according to Abigail, a shot was
fired after you found her in the woods
last night. Can you corroborate?

NOLAN

Abigail said that?

[pause]

She's wrong. The shot didn't come while we were together.

[pause]

I know because *I* fired the shot. I fired at the bigfoot.

Earlier, after the episode with Maylee shooting the gun, I
somehow end up with it. I stash it in my tent to get it away from
her. Then I kind of forget about it—until I go into the woods
looking for everyone. I take it with me, just in case.

When I'm out there, when I see the bigfoot, I totally freeze up. I'm watching it devour Maylee's body, and, look, this creature has to be four hundred pounds. I know very well that Maylee's not exactly going to sustain it. Which means, guess who's going to be the main course? But I still don't move.

And isn't that the exact useless response people would expect from me? Just *standing* there, waiting to be ripped apart. Too scared to even try to fight it because it's easier to lie down and die. I'm pathetic. *Pathetic.*

Then I kind of snap out of it. I'm like, *no.* That's *not* the person I'm going to be. It's too late to help Maylee, but I can save myself and the others. And maybe I can scare the bigfoot away from Maylee's body because... Shit, this sounds morbid, but I'm thinking the police could come later and recover whatever's left. Probably her family would want something to bury.

So I shove my phone into my pocket and wrap both hands around the gun, just like Ray taught me. I fire once. Even in the dark, even though I'm wobbly, I hit the bigfoot. I see the way it falls back.

The words of Grover Krantz are running through my mind, the way he said if he ever shot a bigfoot, the first thing he'd do is reload. I fire again. There's only a click. Then another. No more bullets. My stomach drops. I'm sure I only *wounded* the bigfoot— but now it knows I'm a threat. Now I've made it angry.

That's when I run.

I drop the gun somewhere in the forest along the way. No idea where. But you already found it, didn't you?

[pause]

What?

[pause]

I don't understand what you're saying.

[pause]

No, it was a bigfoot I shot at. I'm sure. Completely sure. There's no way... It couldn't have been a person. It was too tall. It was covered in fur. It was...

Look, I know you don't think bigfoots are real, but they *are*, okay? Even Jane Goodall says they could be real. There are pictographs going back one thousand years that depict them— haven't you ever heard of Tule River? Did you know that when Mount St. Helens erupted in 1980, people saw military helicopters airlifting dead bigfoots out of the forest? There have been sightings in every state but Hawaii. In 19—

What?

[pause]

I'm not upset. I'm just telling you there's evidence. Don't you see that? Bigfoots exist—*lots* of people know bigfoots exist. And there was one at Salvation Creek last night.

Why are you looking at me like that?

There *was*.

I shot a bigfoot, not a person. I wouldn't make that mistake. *No one* could make that mistake.

I'm telling you. That's the truth. I didn't shoot Maylee.

54

Let's take a minute to calm down. Are you
doing okay? Whenever you're ready, tell
us how you decided to leave the forest.

ABIGAIL

I...I can't remember, exactly.

NOLAN

I don't know. Why does it even matter?

Petra wanted to stay to look for Maylee. John was scared
out of his mind, begging us to get out of there. He had the
right idea. I wanted to put as much distance between us
and Salvation Creek as possible before the bigfoot came for
us, too.

There *was* a bigfoot out there.

I saw it.

JOHN

My whole body was shaking—my teeth were chattering even though I didn't feel cold. I couldn't concentrate on anything. My brain skipped back and forth between trying to comprehend that Maylee was dead and trying to figure out how to get the hell out of the woods as fast as possible.

PETRA

Everyone was hysterical. Someone needed to take charge, and it clearly wasn't going to be any of them.

ABIGAIL

I know at one point Petra said, "We need to find Maylee. Abigail, go back to the cabin and search the perimeter. If Maylee's not there, wait for her. Odds are that's where she'll show up. John, you go back to the campsite. Nolan, call 911."

Nolan pointed out that we didn't have cell service.

Petra gave him the meanest look and said, "Oh my God, then drive down the road until you *do*. Do I have to plan everything?"

JOHN

I couldn't tell Petra that Maylee was dead. I needed to, but I couldn't. I knew it would ruin her as much as it ruined me.

Say what you will about Petra, but she's always been loyal to Maylee. She's the type of friend everyone should hope to have.

NOLAN

I didn't shoot Maylee.

Maylee was killed by a bigfoot.

End of story.

PETRA

No one moved. They all stared at me with wide eyes. I shined my flashlight around the group and said, "What's wrong with all of you?"

They were silent. A minute ago they'd been shouting about gunshots and Bigfoot and serial killers. But suddenly no one wanted to say a thing.

ABIGAIL

What was there to say?

Finally, Petra was like, "Fine, I'll go look for Maylee by myself."

She started to stomp back into the woods. John shouted *no*, but Nolan was the one who stepped forward and stopped her.

NOLAN

There was a fucking dangerous animal in the woods. Of course

I stopped Petra from going in. I blocked her way, and when she tried to bust past me, wrapped my arms around her. I kept telling her I wouldn't let her kill herself.

Even though Petra is stronger than me, she didn't break free. Finally, she stopped struggling. I felt her shoulders heaving. She was crying. I started crying, too.

JOHN

It was the thunder that finally convinced Petra to leave. She said rain would wash away Maylee's trail, that we'd never be able to find her. I told her we should call the police immediately, then.

We didn't take anything from the campsite. We left it exactly as it had been earlier that night when there were still five of us.

PETRA

We needed SAR in the woods before the rain started. That's what I kept telling myself. The best thing we could do for Maylee was call the police. So we walked through the woods until Abigail saw a rock formation she remembered and led us back to the campsite. We were actually much closer than I'd realized.

Abigail only agreed to get in the car if John drove—that way she'd be able to see his hands at all times.

John said, "If I killed Maylee, I wouldn't be driving us to a police station right now."

It didn't matter to Abigail. She was already convinced.

John kept shivering, even when we got in the car and turned the heat up. I vaguely remembered something from my SAR class about that being a sign of shock. As we drove down the dirt road, he started crying—not sobs but silent tears that Nolan and Abigail probably didn't notice from the back seat.

I knew he wasn't okay to drive, and normally I'd never stay in a car with an unsafe driver.

But at the moment, *none* of us were okay.

ABIGAIL

We drove just far enough to get service. Petra was the one who made the call. She said, "I need to report a missing person."

Missing, not dead.

My heart broke for her.

NOLAN

On the phone, Petra says, "I'm calling about a missing person."

She's so fucking stubborn. I'm just saying, it doesn't matter who tells her that Maylee is dead, she'll just go on believing what she believes until the very end.

JOHN

Petra reported Maylee missing. I opened my mouth to tell her

Maylee was dead, but I couldn't. I tried the whole drive here. But I knew, once I said those words, there was no going back. Nothing would ever be the same.

55

It looks like something's bothering you.

ABIGAIL

It's just...

NOLAN

Yeah, I have a question, actually.

JOHN

There's one thing that doesn't make sense to me.

ABIGAIL

If John killed Maylee near our campsite...

JOHN

Where exactly did you say Maylee was found again?

NOLAN

Earlier you said Maylee's body was shoved between rocks or something. What was it, like five miles from where I saw the bigfoot kill her?

ABIGAIL

I know time was moving strangely out there in the woods. But...I just don't know how John would have had time to move Maylee's body.

56

Petra, we have an important question. The
others said you refused to leave Salvation
Creek because you wanted to keep searching for Maylee. Why would you have done
that if, to the best of your knowledge, she was still at the cabin?

PETRA

Oh, so you're finally going to use your deductive skills? Well,
good job, detectives, you caught me. I left out some details
earlier, okay?

[pause]

God, yes, I'm going to tell you now. Give me a freaking chance
to take a breath.

[pause]

Maylee and I fought, like I said. She tried to keep me at the cabin and I ran. All of that was true. But I didn't mention that when I left...Maylee followed me. She followed me into the woods.

I was faster than her. I was more comfortable with the terrain, and I was wearing better shoes for it. She didn't even have a flashlight with her, okay? It was pitch-black, and I knew she didn't have a flashlight.

It didn't take long for me to get ahead of her. She shouted at me the whole time. At first it was angry, demanding that I come back, saying stuff like, "For once in your life don't be such a sanctimonious bitch." Around the time I crossed the creek, her voice was more distant, and I could tell she was getting nervous. She pleaded for me to wait for her so we could talk through everything. She said she could explain

But I kept going. I was so mad and hurt that I could barely think. And though I hate to admit it, I was afraid of her, too. What would she do if she caught up to me and I still insisted on going to the police? How far would she go to keep me quiet?

From behind me there was a strange noise—a noise that didn't quite register at the moment—and then Maylee called once more. Just my name. "Petra!" And this time she sounded different. More fearful. But I still kept walking.

I stopped at the rock, just like I told you. I cried for a long time. Then I noticed that Maylee had fallen silent. She wasn't shouting for me anymore. I couldn't hear her following me. That's when I...

[pause]

Oh God.

[pause]

That's when I realized the weird sound I heard, right before Maylee called for me the last time... It was a splash.

She must have slipped on those mossy rocks while trying to cross the creek. She'd nearly slipped when we'd crossed during the day.

I turned around right away. Of course I did. I'm not evil, okay? I turned around as soon as I realized what had happened. I was so mad at myself because the splash should have gotten my attention immediately. It would have if I hadn't been so overwhelmed by my feelings.

I hurried back to the creek. Part of me... Part of me was terrified I'd see Maylee's body floating there. It wasn't. But there were footprints, big soggy footprints coming out of the water.

She'd fallen in. She must have been soaking wet.

I assumed she'd head for the cabin. That would be the logical thing to do. The cabin was warm. It had dry clothes. There was no way Maylee would try to make it back to the campsite.

So I went to the cabin, running the whole way. Inside, it was warm from the wood stove and lit by the glow of lanterns. But it was empty.

Maylee was walking through the woods alone, no flashlight, no sense of direction, in wet clothes. And it was my fault. It was all my fault. If I had gone back when I heard the splash... If I had just agreed to her ridiculous scheme. If I had done any small thing differently, Maylee wouldn't have been in that position. I had to find her. There was no way she could survive on her own.

I went back across the creek. When I heard raised voices, I hoped it might be Maylee. Maybe she'd found John. So I ran through the trees into a clearing. John was bent over vomiting. Nolan and Abigail were crying and shouting—I didn't understand why they were in the woods and not at the campsite. There was no sign of Maylee.

I kept telling everyone we needed to find her, we needed to find her right away, the situation had gone from troubling to dire. We needed to get to Maylee *fast*. It wasn't a cold night, but when you add in the icy creek water... I knew it wouldn't take long for hypothermia to set in.

[pause]

Will you tell me that, at least?

Did Maylee die from the gunshot wound, or did she die of hypothermia?

Please. I've answered all your questions. I've tried to be honest. I've done everything you asked. At least tell me this.

57

We know you want answers. You need
to understand that there are some
things we have to keep to ourselves.
But we'll tell you what we can.

JOHN

       [long pause]

Wait... Preliminary examination confirms *what*?

ABIGAIL

The bullet wound wasn't lethal? I'm sorry, I don't understand...
Then how did Maylee die?

NOLAN

What does hypothermia have to do with any of this?

PETRA

I knew it as soon as you said she was wedged between boulders.

Hide and die.

ABIGAIL

You're saying Maylee fell into the creek before being shot? And then she... She tried to make it back to camp with a bleeding shoulder and freezing clothes until finally...

[pause]

She just curled up somewhere and died?

[pause]

It's so much worse than I imagined.

JOHN

But if all that's true, it means...

NOLAN

There *was* a bigfoot. I... I'm sorry. Say what you will about bullet wounds and hypothermia. I know what I saw.

JOHN

It means when I was leaning over Maylee, she was still alive.

ABIGAIL

But Maylee *was* shot, right? John shot her. She may have died of hypothermia, but John shot her first, because I *heard* it.

[pause]

Except now you're making me unsure of *when* I heard it. Was it when Nolan and I were together or before then?

[pause]

Now that I'm thinking about it, didn't *Nolan* end up with the gun back at the campsite? Did John ever have it at all?

[pause]

And what about the blood on his hands? I could have sworn there was blood. But it was so dark, and later, when I looked closer, his hands were clean. Did I...

[pause]

No, I'm just... I'm just trying to remember.

[pause]

I...

[pause]

I think I might have made a terrible mistake.

JOHN

I'd like to ask you something. If I would have carried Maylee to the car instead of leaving her in the woods, if I would have driven her back to town right away, would she have lived?

[pause]

Right. I guess you wouldn't know that.

PETRA

But, okay, Maylee's cause of death doesn't change the fact that someone shot her. I want to know who it was.

You're not going to tell me, are you?

[pause]

I mean, I know it wasn't me. And it probably wasn't John. The more I think about it, the more sure I am. He wouldn't have touched the gun. He *hates* guns. So that leaves Abigail or Nolan, and I want to say it was Abigail, but...

[pause]

But Nolan was so drunk and so scared.

[pause]

He didn't.

[pause]

Did he?

NOLAN

You're telling me that slopping sound I heard wasn't Maylee being eaten, it was her taking off her wet shoes and socks and throwing them on the ground?

No, I'm sorry.

It doesn't make sense.

ABIGAIL

I need to talk to John. I need to... Should I apologize?

Or would that make everything worse? You know how sometimes you apologize to someone or come clean about something, but it's really for *you*, not them?

[pause]

If he was innocent the whole time, and I stood there and accused him of... I just, I can't imagine how much that hurt. And it got him in trouble, didn't it? When the four of us first got here and told you how Maylee disappeared, you didn't separate us until *I* said...

[pause]

But he *did* have blood on his hands. I really thought he did.
And that's the only reason I suspected him. It didn't have anything
to do with the accident last year. I mean, my dad *is* friends with
Andy Snyder's mom, and I *did* overhear them talking...

I knew those rumors had been disproven, though. I knew
John hadn't done anything wrong. I didn't go into the camping
trip thinking he was a criminal.

[pause]

Did I?

[long pause]

I'm sorry, I just... I don't know. There's a lot I need to think
about.

JOHN
You're saying... What? Abigail is recanting her accusation?

[pause]

I see.

[pause]

I don't know what you want me to do with this. Shrug it off and call it an honest mistake? Why's it always my job to forgive people?

PETRA

Has my brother asked for an attorney? Are you questioning him alone? You need to stop right now. The second my dad gets back from Salvation Creek—the *second*—you need to get him in that room with Nolan.

NOLAN

[long pause]

There *was* a creature, wasn't there?

You've checked the woods, right?

You've looked for some sign of it? Footprints or primitive structures? Even just gouges on trees?

Please, tell me you've found some sign.

EPILOGUE

You've been very helpful. We appreciate you answering our questions so honestly—we know how difficult this has been.

PETRA

My dad says that families of victims always want closure. He
never knows how to tell them they won't get it. They might get
resolution, but not closure.

I guess I understand what he means now.

ABIGAIL

I keep thinking of how things could have happened different.

What if Petra hadn't looked for Maylee until morning? What
if Nolan hadn't brought his thermal imager? What if I'd never
agreed to Maylee's plan in the first place? It's like all these things
had to line up exactly right. If one of them had changed, just *one*,
Maylee wouldn't have ended up alone in the woods, cold and
lost and bleeding.

She must have been so scared.

JOHN

I guess the one comfort—if you can call it that—is that Maylee probably wasn't scared. She's the most fearless person I've ever met. Even if she knew was about to... If she knew how much danger she was in, she would have faced it head-on. She would have been courageous until the very end.

PETRA

I doubt Maylee realized she was going to die.

Knowing her, she was stumbling through the forest with a freaking gunshot wound, thinking it would make a great story for her followers. She wouldn't have even considered how wrong things might go.

It must be better that way, don't you think? Feeling certain until the very last second that you'll be saved.

[pause]

Or maybe that's wishful thinking. Maybe I'm just desperate to believe Maylee had some peace at the end.

Isn't it funny, the things people can convince themselves of?

NOLAN

Can I just...

[pause]

I...

[pause]

There wasn't a bigfoot, was there?

There wasn't anything in the forest but us.

ABIGAIL

I have one more question, if you don't mind. It's probably selfish to even bring this up, but I have to ask anyhow.

I... No, *we*—we all messed up really bad, didn't we?

[pause]

No, that's not the question. Does that count as a question? It was a question before the real question.

The real question is: What's going to happen to us now?

PETRA

Now that you've got the whole story, are you done being cagey? Because I'd like to know if any charges are being pressed—and before you decide, you should think really hard about whether you have a case against Nolan.

Keep in mind that Maylee got him drunk. She got him riled up about Bigfoot. She basically put a gun in his hands. She turned Nolan into a freaking weapon, okay? And you have three people who will testify to that.

Plus, the gunshot wasn't fatal. You said that yourself. So if you're going for manslaughter—

[pause]

Oh. So, like...criminal negligence or something? Considering that he's a juvenile and this is his first offense, it'll probably be a misdemeanor charge. A year of probation, maybe? He'll—

What?

[pause]

God, I *know* you can't answer any of this. I'm thinking out loud, okay?

NOLAN

I was sure of what I saw.

So sure of it.

The bigfoot was real to me. You get that, right? I *saw*—

[pause]

What?

My mom and Ray are here?

[pause]

Yeah, of course I want to see them. I just, well...do they know
what happened? What I did?

[pause]

Not yet.

Okay.

Do you think... Can you let me be the one to tell them?

I feel like it should come from me.

JOHN

That's it? I can leave?

No, I... I don't know what I expected.

[pause]

Do you have my phone? Because I need to call Maylee's
mom. I want to ask if there's anything I can do. Help with...
arrangements or something. I don't know, I just—

[pause]

It's at the front desk? All right. Great. Thanks.

I guess that's it, then.

[stands]

I really did love her, you know.

I just wanted to say that.

ABIGAIL

I can just walk right out? Are you sure?

[pause]

Yes, I *want* to leave. It just seems weird, I guess. Am I supposed to go back to Sunny Acres like nothing happened?

[pause]

After everything I told you, you probably think Maylee is awful, don't you? Her and me both. I wish you could know all the good things about her. I wish the whole world could. Because as Nana Abbie says—

Huh?

[pause]

Right. Sorry.

It's just kinda hard to stop talking after I've been talking for so many hours, you know? But anyhow, I guess I'll go now.

PETRA

We're done here, then?

Okay. Great.

[stands]

Actually.

[pause]

I'm not done.

[sits back down]

Let's talk about Maylee's phone. Have you recovered it yet? It was in her and John's tent last I saw. This is probably going to be a hard no, but is there any chance I could use it for a minute?

[pause]

Why?

Not that it's any of your business, but there are some photos I need to get.

Next up: What time is it? Because it feels really late, and if you want to get Maylee's death on tonight's news, you'll have to hurry. Do you want me to go over the details of her plan again? Or I can talk to the press myself, if you prefer.

Why are you looking at me like that?

You think I'm being callous? Guess again.

Maylee Hayes was my best friend. Was she perfect? No. Did she mess up big-time? Obviously. But that doesn't erase thirteen years of friendship, okay? She's the only person in the world who knew everything about me and loved me anyway—so I'm not going to toss her aside because I saw a part of her personality that I didn't like.

Which all goes to say, right now I'm going to do what Maylee would've wanted me to. I'm going to follow through with her plan.

[pause]

God, no, not *exactly* as she'd intended it. How would that even work?

This is the revised plan—because let's face it: Maylee's plan was flawed from the start. She thought disappearing and coming back would make her famous. But realistically, what would have happened if she managed to pull it off? How long would people have actually cared about her once she was rescued from the woods? A few weeks, maybe? Just until another pretty girl disappeared.

But what *actually* happened—a girl trying to fake her own

disappearance for social media fame and dying in the process? *That's* not an everyday disappearance. *That's* a story that'll be shared and re-shared forever.

Do you know how much shock and outrage this will cause? People will hate-read articles about Maylee. They'll examine every word and picture she's ever put online just to find new reasons to despise her.

And that's precisely what Maylee would have wanted. She didn't care if she was loved or hated. She just wanted to be a legend.

I'm going to make her one.

ACKNOWLEDGMENTS

Writing a book isn't exactly getting lost in the woods, but it can feel like a survival situation all the same. I was fortunate to have a group of brilliant, fearless people navigating the wilderness with me. Thank you to:

My agent, Suzie Townsend, who forever goes above and beyond, improving both my books and the experience of writing them. Sophia Ramos, Kendra Coet, Veronica Grijalva, Victoria Henderson, Pouya Shahbazian, Katherine Curtis and all the hardworking, talented people at New Leaf.

Eliza Swift, my editor, for seeing something special in a two-line concept and helping transform it into a coherent story. The entire Sourcebooks team for bringing passion to every project they undertake.

My early readers who corrected mistakes, untangled plotlines, and forced me to be a better writer: Anna Priemaza, Marley Teter (whose name I'm spelling right this time), Jo Fenning, Josh Hlibichuk, Kristine Kim, Jilly Gagnon, Lana Harper, Adriana Mather, Veronica Klash, Elizabeth Kite, Gordon Brown, Mandy Holland, and Chris Helsabeck.

Dr. Perry whose valuable insights helped bring John to life, making both the character and his situation more realistic and interesting.

Ms. Holland's 2020/2021 creative writing class at Southeast Career Technical Academy for bolstering me with their enthusiasm and smart feedback.

My writing community, those I've already mentioned plus Tasha Christensen, Greg Andree, Katelyn Larson, Annie Cosby, Rachel Foster, Jess Flint, Katie Doyle, Leann Orris, and Morgan Messing for inspiring and entertaining me every day.

Finally, my family—especially Steve Phillips—for the constant love, support, and understanding. They are what makes it possible to keep telling stories.

ABOUT THE AUTHOR

Chelsea Sedoti fell in love with writing when she discovered that making up stories was more fun than doing her schoolwork. (Her teachers didn't always appreciate this.) She now focuses that passion by writing about flawed teenagers who are afraid of growing up, like in her previous novels, *The Hundred Lies of Lizzie Lovett* and *As You Wish*. She lives in Las Vegas, Nevada, where she avoids casinos but loves roaming the Mojave Desert. Visit her at chelseasedoti.com.

sourcebooks
fire

Home of the hottest trends in YA!

Visit us online and
sign up for our newsletter at
FIREreads.com

· ·

Follow
@sourcebooksfire
online